First Daughter

★

White House
Rules

First

Dutton
Children's
Books

Daughter

White House
Rules

★ ★ ★

MITALI

PERKINS

★ ★ ★

Dutton Children's Books | *A division of Penguin Young Readers Group*

PUBLISHED BY THE PENGUIN GROUP

Penguin Group (USA) Inc., 375 Hudson Street, New York, New York 10014, U.S.A. • Penguin Group
(Canada), 90 Eglinton Avenue East, Suite 700, Toronto, Ontario, Canada M4P 2Y3 (a division of Pearson
Penguin Canada Inc.) • Penguin Books Ltd, 80 Strand, London WC2R 0RL, England • Penguin Ireland,
25 St Stephen's Green, Dublin 2, Ireland (a division of Penguin Books Ltd) / Penguin Group (Australia),
250 Camberwell Road, Camberwell, Victoria 3124, Australia (a division of Pearson Australia Group
Pty Ltd) • Penguin Books India Pvt Ltd, 11 Community Centre, Panchsheel Park, New Delhi – 110 017,
India • Penguin Group (NZ), 67 Apollo Drive, Rosedale, North Shore 0632, New Zealand
(a division of Pearson New Zealand Ltd) • Penguin Books (South Africa) (Pty) Ltd, 24 Sturdee Avenue,
Rosebank, Johannesburg 2196, South Africa
Penguin Books Ltd, Registered Offices: 80 Strand, London WC2R 0RL, England

The poem on page 56 is reprinted with permission of Scribner, an imprint of Simon & Schuster Adult
Publishing Group, from THE COLLECTED POEMS OF SARA TEASDALE. Copyright © 1926 by
The Macmillan Company; copyright renewed © 1954 by Mamie T. Wheless. All rights reserved.

CIP Data is available.

Published in the United States by Dutton Children's Books,
a division of Penguin Young Readers Group, 345 Hudson Street, New York, New York 10014
www.penguin.com/youngreaders

Designed by Heather Wood

Printed in USA   First Edition
ISBN 978-0-525-47951-2
1   3   5   7   9   10   8   6   4   2

For James

I'm grateful for Laura Rennert, my sizzling agent,
who helped to envision these books,
and Margaret Woollatt, editor extraordinaire,
who was pre-ordained to work with me on them.

First Daughter

★

White House
Rules

chapter 1

Sameera checked her watch again. Bobby should be making it through security right about now. They'd coordinated their home-for-the-holidays travel plans like spies on a mission, so that Bobby's flight to South Carolina departed ten minutes before Sameera's chartered flight to Ohio. They were hoping to have at least an hour or so together; he was supposed to call from right outside the Private V.I.P. lounge, where the Rightons were waiting.

Pacing past the goodie-laden table, Sameera popped a square of cheddar in her mouth. Then she wished she hadn't. Aged cheese might make her breath smell like one of her grandfather's sick cows. It wouldn't do to remind Bobby of ancient Holsteins when—if—their lips finally met for the first time. Quickly, she opened a soda and swished a sip around her mouth before swallowing.

Next, she took mental stock of her outer self—jeans

3

and high-heeled boots that made her legs look longer, crisp white shirt, brown leather jacket that flared slightly at the waist, light dose of rose-geranium perfume, and a pair of copper earrings that he'd once complimented dangling against her shining black hair. *I'm ready on the outside,* she thought. *If only my adrenaline wasn't pumping like I've had five cappuccinos with extra shots.*

It was time to shatter the strange barrier that had been keeping their friendship from shifting into romance. While they were dancing an inch away from each other on the bhangra floor, chemical undercurrents pulled every cell in her body his way. Couldn't he feel them, too? Or was he just being a kind "South Asian big brother," helping out a "sister" who would have otherwise been totally lonely and bored in D.C. during her father's campaign?

He really isn't that much older than me, Sameera thought. Even though he was a sophomore in college, Bobby had skipped a grade in elementary school, so he was eighteen. And, even though she was technically still a junior in high school, she'd be turning seventeen in just a few months.

"Share the protein, Sparrow," her mother called from across the room. "I can't be responsible for what comes out of my mouth when I'm famished. Feed your dad first, though, will you?"

Sameera filled two small china plates and handed one to her father. President-elect James Righton was standing by the floor-to-ceiling window that overlooked the tarmac, talking to his campaign manager and two other staffers. He smiled his thanks as he accepted the plate and immediately passed it around to the others.

First-Lady-to-Be Elizabeth Campbell Righton was relaxing in a plush armchair, her tired feet propped up on a table. "Thanks, sweetheart," she said, taking the plate. "I'm so glad your father and I are finally getting to meet Bobby."

Her parents hadn't been around the few times Bobby had come over during the campaign. "Yeah, me too, Mom," Sameera answered, trying to fake some enthusiasm.

She *was* glad to get the introduction over with, but she and Bobby would only get about an hour of privacy. *If you can call it that*, she thought glumly, glancing around. The crowded lounge was crammed with talkative campaign staffers still giddy from her father's win, most of them busily planning his inauguration and other festivities scheduled for January. A pair of Secret Service agents, who had been guarding the candidate for weeks now, silently watched from a corner of the room.

Sameera's cell phone played Bobby's ring tone (the theme from *Casablanca*), and she fumbled to open it. "Hi, Bobby. You're here. Great. I'll buzz you in."

Mom was sitting up and easing her shoes back on. "I'll lure your dad away from his groupies," she promised.

Sameera had primed the security guard, so all she had to do was nod for the doors to slide open and make Bobby Ghosh appear like a genie. They'd seen each other a few days before at the Revolutionary Café, but she feasted her eyes yet again on that drop-dead combo of curly black hair, brown skin, white teeth, faded jeans, and oh, those silver bangles with their signature clinking.

"Sameera," he said quietly, stepping into the room. She loved how he used her real name instead of Sparrow, the nickname that had clung to her since her adoption.

Instantly, Sameera was flanked by Secret Service agents. "I'll have to take your bag, sir," the younger one said.

"But he's already been through security," Sameera answered.

"I'm sorry, miss," the agent said. "It's protocol."

Sameera frowned. This was one of those obey-the-rules kind of words she'd started hearing a lot since her father won the election—protocol, tradition, custom, convention, *modus operandi*, procedure. *First Daughter To-Do List,* she thought, as Bobby handed over his bag. *Item One. Figure out my own way to play by the rules.*

She led Bobby to where her parents were waiting, watching a little anxiously as he smiled and shook their hands. At first, it was almost like the three of them were delivering lines from a script she'd written herself.

"We're certainly grateful for the way you and your friends welcomed Sparrow into that South Asian Republican Students' Association of yours," Dad said, showing off his ability to remember details. "Especially since she's not even in college yet. Thanks for your support during the campaign."

"It was our privilege, sir. Even though I'm not sure how

much we accomplished with only four members. Sameera's got honorary status until she joins us at GW."

Sameera shifted her weight from one boot to the other; she hadn't informed her parents that George Washington University had replaced Ohio State at the top of her list of college choices. Her father raised his eyebrows and glanced at her mother but didn't say anything. *Thanks, Dad,* Sameera thought gratefully. He had a stellar track record of not embarrassing his daughter in public.

Mom, though, was no trained diplomat. "So, Bobby, are you Hindu or Muslim?" she asked.

Sameera couldn't believe her ears. Her mother was still clutching her full plate of protein; obviously she hadn't gotten around to taking a bite.

"Er . . . my parents are Hindus," Bobby answered. "But I'm still . . . seeking. On a spiritual journey, I guess."

"Wonderful. We'll have to talk more about that," Mom said.

Not right now you won't, Sameera thought, folding her arms across her chest.

Elizabeth Campbell Righton caught sight of her daughter's expression, winced, and immediately stuffed a tiny sausage into her mouth. Followed by another.

Good. She gets the message. "Is it okay if Bobby and I walk around the airport till it's time to board?" Sameera asked.

Dad shook his head doubtfully. "I don't know, Sparrow. Maybe we should stick together."

"Come on, James," Mom said, obviously trying to recover

ground with her daughter. "What could happen? This is probably the last time we'll be in a public airport for years."

"Well, as long as you stay in sight of your agent. It was good to meet you, Bobby."

"Likewise, sir. We'll have that talk soon, Mrs. Righton."

Bobby barely had time to grab his backpack before Sameera hurried him out of the lounge.

chapter 2

Finally. They were alone. *Well, if you don't count the dude assigned to shadow us and a gazillion holiday travelers waiting to board their planes,* Sameera thought. As far as the eye could see, waiting people were reading newspapers, frowning at their laptop screens, chasing toddlers, or catching up on sleep in uncomfortable sitting positions. The agent was keeping his distance, but she could tell he was watching.

"Sorry about the spiritual interrogation, Bobby," she said, as they boarded a walking escalator and leaned against the moving handrail. "When Mom's burned out, she says anything that pops into her head."

"Didn't bother me," Bobby answered. "I'm sure they're sick of making small talk with strangers. Running—and winning—a presidential campaign has got to be one of the most exhausting activities on the planet."

"We're so looking forward to relaxing on the farm," she said, relieved that he understood. "Dad plays hours of bridge with my uncle and grandparents. Mom curls up on the couch, eats chocolate, and reads 'inspirational' novels. And I get to watch unlimited movies and eat all the fresh-baked cookies I want."

"When do you move into the White House?" he asked.

"Right after the inauguration. I can't wait! And Ran's coming back with us."

"That's great, Sparrow. How long is she going to stay?"

"Until June. And only because Mrs. Mathews, our house-keeper from Brussels, is coming to help out at Merry Dude Dairy Farm. Which, by the way, I still can't believe it's called."

"Doesn't *meri dudh* mean 'my milk' in Hindi?" he asked, as the walking escalator dumped them off.

Sameera almost tripped, and Bobby took her hand to steady her. It was the first time he'd done that, and he didn't let go even though she regained her balance.

"Yeah. And in Urdu, too," Sameera said, relishing the feel of his strong fingers interlaced with hers. One steel bangle brushed lightly against the inside of her wrist. *This is so not the way a brother holds a sister's hand,* she thought, hopes rising by the minute.

"Why in the world did they name it that? I bet nobody for miles around understands a word of either language."

"You're right. But the family was on the hunt to replace The Campbell Family Farm, which we all agreed was boring, so I suggested the phrase as a joke. Of course, they loved it, and now the milk they send everywhere travels in trucks labeled MERRY DUDE DAIRY FARM in English *and* MERI DUDH FARM in Urdu." *They accepted that name almost as quickly as they accepted me,* Sameera thought. She'd been lavished with affection and adored by her mother's family since the day she was adopted.

"Your cousin must do a lot of work on the farm if your parents had to hire a full-time housekeeper to take her place."

"She does. And if she leaves without a sub, our grandmother might be tempted to go back to working twenty-four/seven. Gran's doing a lot better, but she's still not supposed to overdo it."

"My *dadu's* sick, too," Bobby said suddenly.

By now, Sameera knew that the word *dadu* meant "grandfather" in Bengali. Even though the Ghosh family had been in the States since he was a baby, Bobby still used Bangla words for his parents, calling them Baba and Ma instead of Dad and Mom. "Does he have heart problems?" she asked.

"Heart, and a whole bunch of other things. Baba's driving himself crazy worrying. I keep telling him there's nothing he can do from halfway around the planet."

"Can't you bring your grandfather to South Carolina?"

"I'm not sure what's going to happen. I just hope my father doesn't have a heart attack from the stress. Are you hungry, Sameera? There's a coffee stand over there."

"Not really," she said. "I know—let's check out that relaxation store. I can smell the candles from here."

Reclining in two massage chairs, they talked nonstop, discussing family dynamics, Sameera's worries about her father becoming the world's number-one target for loonies with guns, and Bobby's hunt for the right major. *It's so easy to be with him,* Sameera thought, pressing the button to make her chair lean back even more. She forgot completely about the agent who was standing at the entrance. They got up only when Bobby noticed an elderly couple waiting patiently near a sign that read FREE CHAIR TRIALS, FIVE MINUTES ONLY PLEASE.

Their next stop was the coffee stand, where Bobby bought three blueberry muffins and offered one to the agent, who finally cracked a smile. Sameera treated all three of them to cappuccinos. The chairs were taken, so Bobby and Sameera sat cross-legged on an empty corner of the carpet to eat and drink. *And be merry,* Sameera thought, wishing the minute hand on her watch would stop galloping.

At a sunglass shack full of cheap designer imitations, Bobby tried on a flashy, oversize gold pair festooned with fake diamonds. "The DJ at that last place we went dancing would love these. They'd match his diamond and gold belly-button ring. Here, Sameera, try these on." He handed her a pair of simple dark glasses. "You're famous now, you know. Shades can hide your secrets from the masses."

She put them on and stared at herself in the mirror. In fifteen minutes she had to be back to board her plane. Time was running out, and they'd chatted about everything except . . . except the one thing she wanted to talk about most.

Make your move, girlfriend, she told herself sternly, yanking off the glasses and turning to face him. "What if you don't want to hide your secrets?" she asked, looking straight into his eyes.

"Then you don't," he said, moving closer and taking both her hands in his.

"No way!"

"It's her!"

"Sparrow Righton!"

Squealing or shrieking in exactly the same high pitch, a herd of Girl Scouts came stampeding toward them. The agent moved fast, arriving to stand right beside Sameera.

"Oh my gosh! It's her! It's really her!"

"Move over. I can't see."

"Autograph! Autograph! Someone get an autograph!"

Bobby dropped Sameera's hands and backed away. She was alone in a jungle of khaki-clad nine-year-olds—and one Secret Service agent. Quickly, she put on the shades Bobby had handed her.

"I'll sign just a few autographs, Bobby," she called, trying to see over the green berets bobbing around her. "It shouldn't take more than a minute or two."

But would it? Sharpie pens paired with random items like socks and stuffed animals were bobbing in front of her face. Some of the girls were so excited they were trying to hand her their boarding passes.

She signed and signed and signed. Then she posed for at least ten photos, smiling with one arm around a Girl Scout and one eye on Bobby, who was half hidden behind the sunglass shack. He was handing the clerk some money, she noticed, probably for the glasses she was still wearing.

"I have to go, girls," Sameera said finally, pushing her way through the crowd of Scouts and hurrying to Bobby.

He handed her a flat, square package wrapped in holiday paper. "My flight's about to board," he said.

"Mine, too. I'll call from Ohio." She pulled out a larger, bulkier gift from her shoulder bag and tried to hand him a twenty-dollar bill to pay him back for the sunglasses.

"Forget about that," he said. "Wear them and think of me."

"There she is! With that guy!"

"Sparrow! Wait for us!" The herd had found her again.

He tucked the package into his backpack, took her hand, and squeezed it, hard. "To be continued," he said, as the Girl Scouts descended again.

She watched him jog over to the gate marked CHARLES-TON, SOUTH CAROLINA, while absentmindedly signing her name across a Barbie doll's plastic face.

"Better hurry, Miss Righton," the agent told her. "We're going to have to pat down everybody getting on that plane with you."

Sameera signed one last T-shirt as she watched Bobby

disappear into the jetway. "Sorry," she told the Scouts. "My flight's leaving soon."

"*Already?*"

"We've got so much to *ask* you. And *tell* you."

"Can we come with you to your gate?"

Sameera glanced at the agent, who shook his head, a bit reluctantly, she noticed. She backed away from her fans' disappointed faces. "Uh, sorry, girls, you can't . . . it's protocol," she said, feeling a twinge of guilt over her own power-mongering.

chapter 3

Four inches of snow blanketed the lawns the day after the First Family moved into the White House. An Austrian entourage was scheduled to arrive for an informal visit, and the new president and First Lady had already been fed, watered, personally trained, adorned, coiffed, and assigned their respective duties for the day. Now they were waiting in the Diplomatic Reception Hall to greet their visitors.

A bevy of broadcasters stood shivering under the South Portico in the brisk January wind. They informed their viewers that First Daughter Sparrow Righton, the pretty, articulate crowd-pleaser, who had stayed by her parents' sides throughout their ten-day presidential inaugural extra-vaganza, was nowhere in sight this morning. Nor was Miranda Campbell, Ohio dairy farmer's daughter and all-American beauty, who was rumored to be hunkering with her cousin inside the White House.

The reporters were right. Sameera and Miranda were sequestered in the cozy Lincoln Sitting Room on the second floor. They were accompanied by the Campbell family yellow Labrador retriever, Jingle, on temporary loan from Merry Dude Dairy Farm.

Sameera went to the window, pulled back the maroon velvet drapes, and took in the Christmas card–like view of frosted trees and gardens and the Washington Monument. The inauguration had been a constant stream of parties, parades, and revelry—fun, fun, fun, from start to finish. And the day before, an armored limo had transported the Righton family and Miranda from the hotel to their new address—1600 Pennsylvania Avenue. Was she really here? Or was she dreaming?

A television camera facing the White House tilted upward, and Sameera shut the drapes quickly. She didn't mind the media attention, but she had no intention of showing up on the front page wearing baggy red-white-and-blue flannel pajamas that had been a Christmas present from her grandparents. She couldn't avoid being the subject of some camera attention, though, because Miranda was filming her with a tiny, state-of-the-art video camera that had been a gift from Sameera and her parents.

"Put that thing down, Ran. You filmed nonstop through the inauguration, and then all day yesterday while we were moving in. Besides, I'm still in my jammies."

"But you look so cute." Miranda herself was wearing an identical pair of pajamas, but while Sameera's were marked PETITE, her cousin's were extra long to accommodate a thirty-five-inch inseam.

Sameera perched in one of the stiff wing chairs by the roaring fire. *You can't relax in furniture like this,* she thought. The previous tenants obviously hadn't used this room as much as the Campbell-Righton cousins planned to.

Miranda pulled the other wing chair closer to the fire and wiggled her toes luxuriously. "This is the life, Sparrow. Fresh sheets and flowers in our rooms every day, hot meals sent up from the kitchen just when we want to eat, our clothes washed, pressed, folded, and put away. And *not a cow in sight!* Thanks to Mrs. Mathews, I get to feel like a princess for six whole months."

"And thanks to the American taxpayers," Sameera added, stretching and yawning. "I'm exhausted."

The night before, after unpacking most of their stuff, the girls stayed up late exploring. They wandered through as many of the 132 rooms as they could, trying to find all thirty-five bathrooms and twenty-eight fireplaces; bowled a couple of games in the single-lane alley; watched portions of *The Sound of Music* in the theater (singing along like they always did); and played pool upstairs in the game room. Once they left the private residence on the second and third floors, a pair of Secret Service guys tracked them like cats on the prowl.

"How do you like the code names the Cougars picked for us?" Miranda asked. "Cougar" was the retaliatory code name the girls were using for the Secret Service agents.

Sameera started Jingle's daily rubdown, making his tail swing back and forth like a conductor's baton. "Dad's is okay. I sort of like Alpha Dog for him. But Dove for Mom? They obviously haven't gotten to know her very well, have they?"

"I like mine," Miranda confessed.

"Yeah, it figures you'd get a sweet name like Peach," Sameera said. "Meanwhile, I get stuck with Peanut."

"I think it's cute, Sparrow."

"Stop with the cute already. Someone on Sparrowblog commented once about how cute I was, and Bobby responded right away with a rant about how petite women are always labeled cute. He was so right. Stuffed animals are cute. And, okay, these pajamas are cute. But a person completely done with puberty should not be called cute."

"Did he call this morning?" Miranda asked. "Or last night?"

Sameera terminated Jingle's massage abruptly. "Nope. I haven't checked my e-mail yet, but I'm not too hopeful. It's like he's disappeared off the face of the earth, Ran." Bobby's total silence since she'd returned from Ohio was the only dark lining on her silver cloud.

"You were so busy with the inauguration, Sparrow. Maybe he was waiting until all that was done."

"Maybe. But I just don't get it—before the holidays we were humming, Ran. We really were. We almost—at the airport—"

"But then those Girl Scouts crashed the party," said her cousin, who knew the whole story. "You talked almost every day during the holidays, right?"

Sameera nodded. "But ever since we got back to D.C., he might be dead for all I know."

"It *is* sort of weird," Ran said. "Because the present he gave you was incredibly romantic."

On Christmas morning in Maryfield, Sameera opened a framed photograph of a sparrow soaring over a canyon. Bobby had obviously taken it himself, because the initials *B.G.* were etched in tiny letters on the bottom-right corner of the photo. After admiring it from every angle and passing it around to her curious family, Sameera cringed at the thought of the generic Vote for Righton sweatshirt that she'd given him.

"He isn't trying to dump me, is he, Ran?" she asked.

Miranda shook her head. "You don't dump a friend with the silent treatment unless you're a jerk. And from what you've told me, Bobby Ghosh is anything but. I know you're worried, Sparrow, but I'm sure the guy's got a reason for his temporary muteness. Now pour me some more of that brew, will you?"

Along with the coffee, the girls were feasting on fresh-baked scones, clotted cream, jam, and chilled orange juice. And milk from Merry Dude Dairy Farm, of course, which was delivered twice a week directly from Ohio and stored in the private family fridge in the Residence. The rest of the breakfast had been wheeled up on a cart by a smiling usher named Jean-Claude, along with a folded copy of the *Washington Post*. Sameera ignored the paper; she got the news on her laptop, which she was itching to open right now.

"Mind if I use my camera again, Sparrow?" Miranda asked suddenly. "I haven't filmed the Residence in daylight yet, and I want to start with this room. The Lincoln Sitting Room. The place where Honest Abe himself came to chill when the Civil War was stressing him out."

"Go ahead, Ran," answered Sameera. "I need to post on Sparrowblog anyway. Maybe then I'll get a comment from him."

It was hard to tell which cousin activated her own techno toy first, but Jingle settled himself on the Persian carpet in front of the fire, knowing he'd be on his own for a while.

chapter 4

Sameera titled her new Sparrowblog post, "Four Things You Might Not Know About the House."

> Lots of you have been wondering what it's like to live in The House that you see on your twenty-dollar bills. Well, here's a rundown so far.

(1) <u>Many people work here</u>. Over one hundred, in fact. Cougars (aka Secret Service dudes) are always on the prowl—a few of them are even on the roof 24/7. They use code names for everything and everybody. I can't tell you what mine is, because if I did, I'd have to kill you. Ran and I came up with our own countercode—so far we have Cougars, Pandas (chefs), Penguins (valets), Orcas (maids in black-and-white uniforms that make them look amazingly killer whaleish, even the skinny ones), Salmon (tourists), Retrievers (Dad's staff), Dolphins (Mom's staff), and Rhinos (paparazzi with huge lenses).

(2) <u>You can break a sweat without leaving the place</u>. Mom, Ran, and I had our first workout yesterday in the gym with Manuel: He Moves You, personal trainer and out-of-shape-body-whisperer. Coxing never pumped the body much, so I'm hoping to display toned triceps the next time the Rhinos catch me sleeveless. Afterward, Ran and I bowled a quick game at the bowling alley, and I got two strikes, thanks to my already strikingly (get it?) enlarged triceps.

(3) <u>There's a big, big screen here</u>. Not only that, but the theater is lined with plush recliners and we get to choose from thousands of flicks, even first-run

feature films BEFORE they hit the theaters. We can order gobs of hot, buttery popcorn from Orcas who are always asking if we need anything. Ran and I got all quiet and nirvanaish when we tiptoed into that red-carpeted, surround-sound shrine of bliss.

(4) The kitchen is a play area. Note to self: when bored, try baking in the White House kitchen with state-of-the-art appliances, unlimited ingredients, and three or four Cordon Bleu Pandas on hand to correct any mistakes. Sadly, Jingle, our farm pooch who's visiting with Ran, is banned from the kitchen. But he gets to sleep on my bed at night. Or do I get to sleep on his bed? It's hard to tell which one of us owns the space, but it's all good.

Comments? Remember, keep them short, clean, and to the point. Peace be with you. Sparrow.

She hit publish, and the post went live, spinning across cyberspace to be read by thousands of Sparrowblog readers around the world.

Next, Sameera skimmed through the dozens of comments on her most recent post about the inauguration festivities, registering another zinger from Sparrowhawk, a frequent visitor who liked to provoke a reaction from her. Comments from critics didn't usually faze Sameera, but for some reason Sparrowhawk's words twisted their way into her mind like an electric screwdriver.

> Listen up, Princess. I just read in the Times that
> you're supposed be some kind of shining example
> for the rest of us teenagers with brown skin. Yeah,
> right. Well, it's clear that YOUR skin is nothing but
> camo for a bunch of white privilege. Private tutor,
> rich parents, servants, parties . . . I'm surprised that
> dog of yours isn't tiny and that you don't carry him
> around in a Gucci bag designed just for him. Why not
> walk in my shoes for a change? Ever had to worry
> about having enough money for groceries? Ever try
> to get a decent education at a school where drug
> deals are happening in the hall? Wake up, birdbrain.
> You wouldn't make it one day in my territory.
> Sparrowhawk.

Sameera couldn't help reading the comment twice, and then again. Was Sparrowhawk right? *Was* she on the verge of becoming a pampered wimp? *I'll deal with you later, Hawk,* she thought, and scrolled through the rest of the comments before checking her e-mail. There was no sign of Ghoshboy anywhere: not on the blog, not on IM, and not in her in-box. But there *was* a note from Mariam, a friend Sameera had made on a day she'd gone shopping incognito for burkas during the campaign. Mariam, like

Sameera, was born in Pakistan. Now she lived with her family in a D.C. neighborhood not far from the White House. She was replying to a letter of apology from Sameera, and her graciousness soothed Sameera's ruffled soul a bit.

```
I'm SO glad you wrote, Sameera, and told us
your real identity. No need to apologize—I
can only imagine the pressure you must have
been facing, and probably still are. You were
so good to my grandmother, and we'll never
forget that. My father says that if your
father is anything like his daughter, this
country is in good hands. I would love to
stay in touch somehow, but I understand if
it's impossible. Peace be with you, too. With
love, Mariam.
```

She would definitely have to invite Mariam over for a visit, Sameera decided. Sangi, founder of the South Asian Republican Students' Association at George Washington University, had also written a note.

```
Sparrow! We're having our first SARSA meeting
of the year this Friday at the Revolutionary
Café. Any chance you could join us? We've all
been missing you, but judging by that sad,
```

distracted expression he gets every time I
mention your name, Mr. Bobby Ghosh is missing
you even more. He definitely doesn't want to
talk about it with me, but I'm sure the sight
of you will cheer him up. Hope you can come.
Sangi for ALL of us.

So he was alive, after all! And "sad and distracted." Well,
why didn't he call then? Something strange was going on,
and she had to find out what. She'd sent her last e-mail
to him about three days ago; it might be okay to risk another one.

Hey, you. I haven't heard from you in
forever. Maybe you've seen one too many of
those movies about presidents' daughters and
their dating traumas. Maybe you don't want
to be hounded by the media and labeled
something horrible like "Sparrow's Southern
Boy Toy." But you might at least answer ONE
of my e-mails or phone calls. Did I just
imagine the spark that sizzled when our eyes
met by the sunglass shack?

Sighing, Sameera dragged this pathetic attempt to communicate into the trash. If Bobby got an emo outpouring
after the deluge of calls and e-mails she'd already sent, he'd

probably contact one of those relationship advice bloggers. In fact, maybe he already had.

> **Q: How do I get rid of a First Daughter Stalker without getting arrested?**
> A: *Ignore her e-mails and phone calls until she gives up on you.*

Sighing, Sameera powered down and tucked her laptop back into its case.

Miranda put down her camera. "Nothing from Bobby?"

"Nope. He's still Claude Rains-ing me." *The Invisible Man* was on her list of top twenty classic black-and-white films. "But Sangi tells me he's alive, at least. She wants me to meet them at the café tomorrow for their meeting."

"That's a great idea! Bobby's probably going to be there, right? It gives you the perfect way to run into him without looking too obvious. And then maybe you can pull him aside and find out what's been going on."

"Yeah, we'll have total privacy, won't we? The two of us; Cougars in suits, earpieces, and sunglasses; and a dozen reporters writing down every word we say. That's probably why he's avoiding me, Ran. It's First Daughter phobia."

"I'll bet you're right, Sparrow! Remember that movie about the First Daughter who couldn't get a date, and that classic *West Wing* episode about the president's daughter getting used by some guy? Maybe he's worried that you'll question his motives now that you're related to the most powerful man on the planet!"

Sameera called Jingle over for some more fur therapy, running her fingers again and again through his soft coat. *Was* the ultimate Southern gentleman backing off because he was intimidated by her new, extremely famous address? He hadn't seemed worried about that when they were saying good-bye at the airport. "Then why didn't he tell me himself? How hard would that have been?"

"Maybe he will when you see him."

"But won't the Cougars and Rhinos freak him out even more?"

The girls were quiet, and Sameera started pacing the room, with Jingle dogging her like a K-9 member of the Secret Service. She stopped suddenly, and Jingle came to a halt beside her, perching on his haunches patiently.

"Okay, here's the plan, Ran," Sameera said. "Tomorrow afternoon, we go to a spa somewhere in the neighborhood and check in."

"Sounds great so far," said Miranda.

Sameera didn't stop: ". . . but instead of getting a two-hour sea-salt wrap and massage, I sneak out the back door and head over to the coffeehouse. Wearing my burka." The woolly winter burka that she'd bought last fall from Uncle Muhammad's shop was carefully folded and stashed in one of her bureau drawers.

"*What?* Are you nuts? You can't do that, Sparrow. Stupid, stupid plan."

But the idea was heating up Sameera's brain like a fever. She *had* to see Bobby again. "Sparrow the First Daughter can't, but Sameera can. Sameera the Pakistani girl, remember? Will you cover for me, Ran?"

Her cousin was shaking her head doubtfully, but before she could answer, a loud rapping came at the door, and Jingle began his usual yip-yip-YIP crescendo of barks.

chapter 5

"Girls! Time for your dance lesson!" Tara Colby called from the hallway.

"Hush up, Jingle," Miranda said, getting up to open the door. "We'll talk about this craziness later, Sparrow. Hi, Ms. Colby."

Tara Colby was an ex-senator's daughter who knew the D.C. social scene well because she'd maneuvered the inner circles her entire life. A type A bundle of energy, she'd relaxed a lot over the course of the campaign. Now she was managing the First Lady's office, handling the details of White House etiquette and entertaining that Elizabeth Campbell Righton despised. Ensconced in an East Wing office right beside the First Lady's, Tara was turning out to be absolutely indispensable, just as Mom had predicted.

The ultimate right-hand woman looked polished and slim in a black power pantsuit and matching pumps, and her eyes raked over the girls' pajamas. "Get ready quickly, girls," she said, her voice as crisp as the collar of her powder-blue blouse. "Your partners are waiting. Bring along the shoes you plan to wear to the ball on Saturday night. Have you decided what you're wearing, Sparrow? You know it's protocol for girls who open a Viennese Ball to wear white."

There was that word again. It was starting to get on Sameera's nerves. "My silk dress is fine with me."

"The one you wore to the father-daughter dance during the campaign? I suppose that will have to do for this event; it's a good thing the only photographs taken will be official ones by our photographer. No press allowed."

"I wish I'd known that *before* I splurged," said Miranda. She'd picked out a not-on-sale designer-label white halter dress and matching pumps from an expensive, trendy boutique. At the time, Sameera had clamped her lips to keep herself from pointing out that her cousin's savings account was about to be depleted, or from offering to pay for the outfit herself.

"Can you dance in those shoes?" Tara asked Miranda. "They're pretty high."

"I hope so. The bigger question is whether or not I can learn to waltz in one afternoon. Sameera already knows how, but it's new to me. I hope I don't look like a total clod on Saturday night."

"There's nothing in the least bit clodlike about you, Miranda," Tara said. She was right. The First Cousin's long, elegant limbs transported her gracefully through a room, even on three-inch heels.

"Besides, I may know the box step, but we're going to have to waltz Viennese-style," Sameera added. "It's way faster—Austrian couples whirl around a ballroom like those teacups at Disneyland."

"Being a part of this opening ceremony is the perfect way to honor your parents' visitors," Tara said. "Besides, wait till you meet the Austrian diplomatic offspring who are going to serve as your dance partners—I think you'll consider them . . . how should I put it? Easy on the eyes?"

"Yes! We desperately need an eye-candy fix," Miranda said.

"What about you, Tara?" Sameera asked. "You haven't dated anybody in a while." Wilder, a temperamental marketing guru who'd been fired by Dad's campaign manager, was Tara's most recent romantic fiasco.

"I'm too busy to date. Now get out of those pajamas, girls, and make it quick."

Still the same Bossy Old Wench, Sameera thought affectionately as she headed into her bedroom to change. *But she's definitely mellowed. Sounds like she could use some help getting over Wilder; Ran and I will have to see what we can do.*

Tara led the girls downstairs to the State Room, where paneled walls, vintage crystal, gleaming floors, mahogany tables, and immense sparkling chandeliers made Sameera feel like Beauty in Disney's animated flick. The two hunks striding over to meet them were far from beasts, however. Tara had been right.

"Grüss Gott," the first one said, bending low over Miranda's hand and kissing it. *"Ich heisse Peter."* He was tall, blond, and broad-shouldered—a perfect match for Sameera's cousin, who was already taking stock of her dance partner from head to toe.

"Hey," Ran breathed, getting his message even though she didn't speak a word of German. "And I'm Miranda."

The slimmer, dark-haired guy shook Sameera's hand. *"Ich heisse Wilhelm,"* he said.

"Und ich heisse Sameera," she answered, grateful that the lessons she'd taken in Brussels allowed her to introduce herself in German—and then inform natives that she couldn't speak their language: *"Ich kann ein bisschen Deutsch, aber nicht so gut."*

Her dance-partner-to-be grinned happily. "Your accent is *sehr gut.* I speak English, but like your German, it is only a sampling. I must call you Sparrow instead of Sameera, though. We have greatly enjoyed the German translation of your blog."

"Thanks." *So they're reading Sparrowblog all the way in Vienna. Wow!*

"You'd better get started," Tara said. She switched on the music and left.

A space had been cleared for them to practice near the fireplace, where an enormous portrait of Abraham Lincoln gazed down at them benevolently. Patiently and politely, the guys explained the steps of the opening routine, which they and six other white-gloved couples would have to pull off. Peter clutched Miranda's waist and Wilhelm encircled Sameera's. Slowly at first, their partners twirled the girls, and then faster and faster.

Wilhelm commented several times on how featherlight Sameera felt in his arms, but Peter looked like he was getting a workout. When they sat down for a rest, her cousin's dance partner mopped his forehead with a napkin and reached for one of the icy Italian lime sodas that Jean-Claude carried in on a silver tray.

Sameera had always enjoyed dancing. "How're you doing?" she asked her cousin.

"Fine when we're the only ones out there," Ran said, panting and fanning herself. "But what about when the entire East Room is full of spinning couples? I hope I don't feel like a bumper car gone wild."

"What do you think of them?" Sameera asked, lowering her voice. Their dance partners were standing by the piano, downing bottles of soda and chatting in French with Jean-Claude, who was originally from Haiti.

"Oh, I adore foreign guys. I fell in love with your entire crew team when I visited you in Brussels last year, remember? What about you?"

Wilhelm had dark, longish hair, an accent, and he was trilingual and courteous—a combo of qualities that were usually alluring to Sameera. Too bad she didn't feel even a twinge of attraction. After years of harboring multiple, simultaneous infatuations, she'd suddenly morphed into a unicrush woman—thanks to an Indian-American college guy in blue jeans and bangles.

"They remind me of my crew guys, too," she said. "Great to be around and always good to watch, but no zing factor for me."

"*I* think they're both hot," Ran said. "I like older people and all, but we haven't schmoozed with *anybody* under the age of twenty since I got to D.C. Other than each other, of course."

"You're right, Ran. We should invite them up for a visit. I was a diplomat's kid, too, remember? It can get lonely when you travel with your parents."

"Now you're talking. Maybe spending time with a couple of European hunks will help you forget the insane idea you came up with to see Bobby."

"It's not insane, Ran," Sameera insisted. "I just need time to figure out the details. But we can't have visitors right now—we'll have to ask them to come back tonight. Designer Danny's coming at two."

"How could I forget *that*? I still can't believe we finally get to meet him."

"Not just meet him. *Decorate* with him, Ran."

"Okay, we'll ask them to come back right after Danny leaves."

Sameera shook her head. "Can't. We've got our first tutoring session with Westfield later this afternoon."

"Wow, it's busy being a First Niece. Tonight, then, and I know the perfect movie. Matt Damon and that hot German girl in *The Bourne Identity*—tons of action and shooting, not much conversation . . . they'll love it."

At first their guests seemed a bit overwhelmed by the private movie invite—especially Wilhelm. *Surprise, surprise,* thought Sameera. *Is there a guy on the planet who wouldn't get freaked out at the thought of a date with a First Daughter?*

"We would be happy to escort you to dinner before the film," Wilhelm said, staging a quick recovery.

The son of a diplomat, definitely, Sameera thought, admiring his skills. "We'll order pizza," she told him. "But come early, because as you know, the pat-down, identity-check security stuff can take a while. And they won't let you in if you bring—"

Miranda chimed in with the White House guest prohibition list: "—any animals (except guide dogs), oversize backpacks, balloons, beverages, chewing gum, electric stun guns, fireworks or firecrackers, food, guns or ammunition, knives with blades over three inches or eight centimeters, mace, nunchakus, cigarettes, or suitcases."

chapter 6

Sameera's mother, who could care less about interior design, had delegated all First Lady redecorating rights to her daughter and niece.

"Pick a good designer, girls," Tara had told them privately. "We've got a bit more money in the budget than your mom realizes."

The girls, of course, had chosen Designer Danny, host of the hit reality show *Décor for Dummies*—one of the cousins' many shared addictions. His people smugly accepted the office of the First Lady's call for help, never dreaming that when Sameera and Miranda suggested his name, Elizabeth Campbell Righton would respond with a baffled, "Who's *he*?"

In addition to getting new furniture for the Lincoln Sitting Room, the cousins were going to redo their bedrooms, the living quarters on Air Force One, and a few rooms at Camp David. They were leaning toward California minimalist on Air Force One, because James Righton liked things streamlined, Ohio-farm cozy in their bedrooms and the Lincoln Room, and global-import-trendy at Camp David, which meant lots of sequins, paisley, silk, mosaic, batik, and squashy ottomans with tassels. But of course they wanted to hear from Designer Danny, too.

The popular host of *Décor for Dummies* was much tinier than he appeared on television—about the same height as Sameera herself. He flitted around the Lincoln Sitting Room like a hummingbird, fingering fabrics and stroking wood, even getting on his hands and knees to squint into the weave of the heirloom Persian carpet. Sadly, his habit of emphasizing certain words turned out to be extremely annoying in real life.

"I'm so *glad* you girls called me in. Redecorating a place like the *White House* will require the *utmost* care and expertise."

"We still haven't figured out a budget for this room," Sameera told him. "But we're hoping at least to buy some comfortable chairs."

"We must have magnificent *traditional* furniture to match the beauty of these architectural lines. For chairs and a settee, I'll need to travel to Italy. France. Maybe Portugal."

"Mom told us to keep it simple," Sameera said sternly, trying to rein him in. "She thinks most of this place is fine the way it is."

"Besides, we were hoping to make this room feel a little more . . . contemporary," Miranda added.

"Oh no, girls. Simple is *not* what this room needs," Danny said with a shudder of distaste. "And definitely not *contemporary*. That *demonstrates* the difference between the *taste* of a novice and the *eye* of an expert. It's a good thing your mother called me."

Sameera could tell that her cousin was just as irritated as

she was by the "novice" comment. They knew how to "respect historical architectural lines"—the marriage between architecture and interior décor was a recurring theme in Danny's show. And just because they were teenagers didn't mean they had bad taste. In fact, they'd had a great time redecorating the family room in their grandparents' house; visitors often commented that the cozy look perfectly reflected the Campbell clan's hospitality. And Sameera had received accolades from the State Department for the job she'd done on the den in the Ambassador's Residence in Brussels.

The girls used up their first expensive hour-long consultation convincing Designer Danny that a pair of comfortable leather recliners by the fire wouldn't wreck the "austere Victorian environment" of the room.

After the session, he headed downstairs, stopping to fondle vases and urns and gaze at paintings that he passed. The cousins watched him go, noting his rapture over the chandelier in the stairwell and the way he caressed the mahogany banister as though it were alive.

"He's a bit too . . . invested, I think," Miranda murmured thoughtfully.

"And he wants to spend oodles of cash. We could have bought one of the recliners we want with the money we owe him for today. I think we'll send a note to his people that the First Lady's all set for now."

"Sounds good." Miranda sighed. "Another idol bites the dust."

Sameera knew exactly what her cousin was talking about. "That jerk from *American Rock Star* tried to get a little too hands-on the other night, didn't he?"

"I shredded his autograph. Thanks for the intervention, by the way."

"Any time. We'd better get ready for school."

They'd decided to use the East Sitting Hall on the second floor as the setting for their tutor's two-hour one-on-one sessions. That way, the other cousin could relax in the adjoining Lincoln Sitting Room doing homework, watching television, or surfing the Web.

That first afternoon of White House school, even with Westfield teaching her as efficiently and patiently as ever, Sameera was distracted. She was eager to figure out her confront-Bobby plan, and for some reason, Sparrowhawk's provocative blog comment kept running through her mind.

"Okay, Sparrow," said Westfield finally. "Say what you have to say, and then we'll get back to geometry. What's up?"

"Don't take this personally, Westfield, because we both know how good you are," Sameera said. "But what do you think about me going to school, for my senior year at least?"

"It's not a bad idea, actually. But would you want to start a new school just for one year? Wouldn't that be hard?"

"Maybe. But I miss being *involved*. In Brussels I coxed for the crew team, helped organize fundraisers for *great* causes, and was probably going to be the *editor* of the paper by my senior year." *I'm emphasizing just like Designer Danny,* she realized. *Maybe it's contagious.*

"I see your point. If you were a normal homeschooler, we could get you involved in group activities and clubs, but you're sort of a special case, aren't you?"

"Now there's an understatement. Other First Kids went to school, right?"

"Yes, but I'm not sure how open your parents would be to the idea, Sparrow," Westfield said. "The world's a much more dangerous place now."

"So I'm supposed to hide inside the White House for four years? No way, Westfield."

"Hey, I'm on your side, Sparrow," the tutor said.

Sameera sighed. "I'll have to use the old make-your-parents-see-the-light family dinner plan."

"Really? And what does that entail?"

"You encourage them to take a nap, promising to organize dinner while they rest. Then you set the table, light some candles, and serve up warm, crusty bread and a great salad. Followed by one of their favorite entrées. You let them relax, eat, drink, laugh, talk. Then, over coffee and dessert, you casually bring up the controversial subject. The plan works best on a Sunday afternoon, by the way."

"You conniving child. Let me know how it goes. Now let's get back to geometry."

During Miranda's turn with Westfield, Sameera scoured

the Web, found the spa closest to the Revolutionary Café, and made reservations for herself and her cousin. She called Tara's office phone, hoping to leave a message asking for a car and a Secret Service detail.

But Tara herself picked up after one ring, and she wasn't thrilled with Sameera's Friday afternoon plans. "Who recommended *that* hole-in-the-wall?" she asked. "There's a fantastic full-service luxury spa in Arlington that caters to political families. I could also set up an appointment for you girls right in the White House."

"I know, but I want this place, Tara," Sameera said firmly. *Next time I'll invite you to join us, because all you do is work 24/7 and you* need *a day at the spa. But not this time.*

"Okay, Sparrow," Tara said, giving up. "I'll have someone make the arrangements."

Wilhelm and Peter arrived on schedule, bearing supersize boxes of sour candies and chocolate-covered raisins for the movie. They happily gave permission for Miranda to film as they oohed and wunderbarred the velour seats and huge screen in the theater. Miranda was also filming (without permission) the Cougars who stood in the back, earpieces in place and sleeve microphones picking up every sound. She turned her camera off only when the lights dimmed, settling into her chair with a squirm of satisfaction.

Sameera noticed that Peter immediately put an arm around her cousin, and that Miranda just as quickly removed it. She sat next to Wilhelm (who maintained a

respectful nontouching distance at all times, thank goodness), barely watching *The Bourne Identity*, which she'd seen
twice already thanks to her cousin's intense Matt Damon
fixation of a few years ago. Politely, Wilhelm tilted the
open candy box in her direction, and Sameera accepted a
sour apple ring, mentally rehearsing the details of her see-
Bobby-again-if-it-kills-me plan.

The first thing she had to do, of course, was convince
her cousin to participate.

"No way, Sparrow," Miranda said again as the girls both
brushed their teeth in Sameera's bathroom that night. Their
guests had left after a rousing bowling competition in the
single-lane alley, with the girls eking out a three-games-to-
two victory.

Sameera rinsed and spit into the basin. "I *promise*, nothing's going to happen to me, Ran. I promise."

"But what if it does? What if you get . . . kidnapped or
something?"

"Nobody gets kidnapped on the spur of the moment,
Ran. Give me some credit, will you? I've been walking
around the streets of big cities by myself for years. You
don't think an American ambassador's kid was a vulnera-
ble target? I knew how to stay safe then, and I know how
to stay safe now. Besides, I'll be in disguise from head to
toe. Please, Ran. All you have to do is hold on to my locator while you have a wonderful, relaxing spa treatment."

"How are you going to ditch the Cougars?"

"Leave that part to me. Just . . . don't blow my cover, okay? And give me two hours. I have to see him, Ran."

Her cousin sighed. "I'm an idiot. I'll do it, but you owe me big-time, Sparrow."

Sameera threw her arms around Miranda. "Thanks, Ran. You won't regret it."

chapter 7

During a tough physics session the next afternoon, Sameera almost wished she *was* getting the lime and Dead Sea–salt scrub she'd reserved. Finally, Westfield left, and it was time to head out.

When the armored black limousine dropped them off in front of the spa, a two-man Cougar team was already there, ready and waiting. Sameera was relieved to see that they had an all-male detail tonight, including the driver. The Cougarette who was sometimes assigned to cover Peanut and Peach could easily have followed the girls into the ladies' locker area. There was no way Sameera wanted close surveillance today.

The driver stayed in the limo, but the youngish agent who'd trailed Sameera and Bobby at the airport (the girls had dubbed him Young Cougar until they got better at names) and his colleague, a middle-aged dude with flecks of gray in his hair (aka Mature Cougar), had to wait in the richly scented reception area, where even the combo of flickering candlelight and soft Peruvian flutes failed to relax them. Tall, vigilant, and stiff, they stood on either side of the front entrance like black pillars.

"My bag is huge," Sameera whispered to Miranda as they stood behind a stressed-out-looking client checking in for a treatment. "Do you think someone will notice?"

"You could be bringing in your own robe or something," Miranda hissed back. She was fumbling in her purse for money.

The only awkwardness between the cousins arose when they had to pay for something. Sameera wasn't an extravagant shopper, but she'd always bought whatever she needed without stopping to think. Miranda's allowance, while perfectly adequate by Maryfield, Ohio, standards, was nothing compared to the generous expense account the Rightons always provided for their daughter.

"Don't be crazy, Ran," Sameera said, pulling out her credit card. "This was my idea."

As her cousin watched, frowning, Sameera added a generous tip for the services she wasn't going to have.

They gathered up their waffle-weave white robes and waterproof slippers and headed for the ladies-only locker room. Just before they left the reception area, Miranda turned to wave at the Cougars. "Have fun," the younger agent called, and Sameera felt a pang of guilt. Here they'd take a bullet on her behalf, and she was planning to trick them.

She'd have to make sure she was back in two hours—without getting caught.

Thankfully, inside the locker room were only a few exhausted women who didn't want to connect with strangers or recognize familiar faces, even famous ones. Nobody paid the slightest attention to anybody else, which was perfect for Sameera's purposes. She stuffed her robe and slippers into a locker, took her bag, and ducked into one of the private dressing rooms.

Miranda's mouth fell open when she came out. "Wow, Sparrow. I've never actually *seen* you in one of those things. You were right—nobody's going to recognize you."

"It's a good thing it's cold outside. I'm sweating up a storm already. And I hope there's a rear service exit from the locker room."

"Be careful, please, Sparrow. I'll leave my cell phone on—call me if you run into trouble."

"You might not be able to answer it while you're getting that wrap. They pretty much swaddle you, I think."

"Well, that'll make two of us, then," Miranda said, fingering the cloth of her cousin's thick head covering.

"Here's my locator." Sameera handed Miranda the small electronic box that a First Daughter was supposed to carry with her at all times.

"I still can't believe you're doing this," Miranda said. She took the locator reluctantly and tucked it into the pocket of her robe.

Sameera leaned forward and kissed her cousin's cheek

through the gauzy fabric of her veil. "Thanks, Ran," she said. "Have fun."

"Yeah, right. I'm going to be in agony till you get back. Here I am at a spa and I'm so not relaxed it's not even funny. Stay safe, Sparrow."

Sameera made her way toward the sound of whirling washers and dryers at the far end of the locker room. Thankfully, no one but her cousin was keeping track of her progress. She slipped out of the back laundry into a service alley and through a door that led to the sidewalk.

Once she was out, Sameera headed quickly away from where the limo was parked. She tried to walk with a middle-aged demure gait. If the Cougar in the driver's seat glanced in his rearview mirror, she wanted him to see the back of a Muslim woman. It was twilight now, and she made sure to stay out of the streetlights, keeping close to the shadows of the buildings.

When she finally turned the corner, she exhaled in relief. She'd done it, thanks to the wonderful burka that she'd bought last August. Well, that she'd been given by the shop owner and his family, actually, during the campaign. *I'll have to visit Uncle Muhammad's shop and actually BUY something this time,* she thought, hurrying toward the Revolutionary Café. *And see Mariam again.*

The SARSA meeting was taking place at a table right by the door. As soon as she walked in, Sameera recognized her friend Sangi's voice booming out as confidently as ever. Sangi's best buddy, George, must have gotten contacts because his glasses were gone. Beside him was the ever-gorgeous Nadia, fiddling with a silken strand of her long, shining hair.

And there *he* was, with his back to her. Quietly, she approached their table, trying to keep her heart from beating visibly through the thick black wool.

"Sparrow?! Is that you?" Sangi asked, and Sameera was grateful that she'd lowered her voice.

Bobby jumped off his chair as though he'd received an intense electric shock. One look into his brown eyes, and the flickers of attraction Sameera had been missing with Wilhelm spontaneously combusted into a raging inferno. But why had he grabbed his backpack as though he were about to make a run for it? And was that an expression of *relief* on his face as his eyes traveled across her burka?

"She came! You were right, Sangi," George said. "She was just telling us that she e-mailed you, Sparrow."

"I didn't think you would," said Nadia. "Can you *be* here alone?"

Bobby didn't say anything, but he sat down again and put his bag on the ground beside him.

"I snuck out," Sameera said. "I had to see . . . you guys. Keep it quiet, will you?"

"Here," George said, pulling up another chair. "I'll get your coffee. Cream, no sugar, right?"

"Right. Thanks." She sat down.

"We weren't sure if they let you mingle with the masses

like this on your own," Sangi said. "Aren't you supposed to have agents protecting you at all times?"

"Yep. I ditched them."

"For us?" Bobby asked, and even though his voice was so low, she could hear the intensity in it.

Courage, Sameera thought. "For you," she said simply, looking him straight in the eyes.

Sangi and Nadia stood up just as George got back with Sameera's coffee. "Here it is," he announced cheerfully, sitting down again on his stool. "So, how have you been, Sparrow? Hey . . . wait a minute . . . I'm not going anywhere. What is *wrong* with you two? We haven't seen Sparrow since . . ."

His voice trailed off as Sangi and Nadia hauled him to the other side of the coffeehouse. Bobby and Sameera were alone.

"I'm so glad you came, Sameera," Bobby said. "I know I need to explain why I haven't answered your phone messages. Or called."

"That's why I'm here," she said, taking a sip of coffee in a superhuman effort to remain calm.

"It's just that when I opened that Vote for Righton T-shirt you gave me, Ma and Baba started asking questions . . . about us."

"What's the problem? Are they Democrats or something? Do they hate my dad?"

"No. They're not even citizens yet. It's something else."

"What? What is it, Bobby? You've got to tell me; we don't have much time."

"*All right*, Sameera. I'm doing my best. I told you my grandfather's really sick back in India, right?"

She nodded.

He took a huge sip of coffee as though trying to steady his nerves with the caffeine. "Well, that's why my parents made me promise not to contact you. They don't want me to be photographed with you in public, because they're afraid he'll see it. And get stressed out."

"But why? He doesn't even know me. Does he hate Americans or something?"

Another enormous chug of coffee. "No, no, not that. It's because . . . because you're Muslim."

She was flabbergasted. "I don't practice Islam."

"Doesn't matter. You're Muslim by birth. And like I told your mom, my family's Hindu."

"And . . . ?"

"So—one of my great-uncles was killed by Muslims during the war. And we lost our jute farm when our village was taken over by Muslims."

"But that was ages ago, Bobby. What does that have to do with me? Or us?"

He frowned into his cup, shifting uncomfortably in his chair, and she finally realized that he was battling immense amounts of embarrassment.

Quickly, she purged any hint of the frustration she was

feeling out of her voice. "I've had friends from lots of cultures and traditions, Bobby. Nothing you say is going to sound strange or weird to me, I promise."

He stopped squirming and sat up a little straighter. "Dadu's got this grudge against the Muslims because of his brother's death, and the jute farm, and with his illness and all . . . well, Ma and Baba think it might kill him if he knew I was seeing you. Or if we were ever photographed together. So they told me not to call or e-mail you."

Sameera thought of her Turkish crew teammate and his Armenian love, whose parents had forbidden them to date. But the two of *them* had met on the sly. "And you promised?" she asked. "Just like that?"

"I had to. They asked me on the way to the airport. Baba was so upset by the latest update on Dadu's health, and Ma was crying. What else could I do?"

You could have said, "No way, this is the twenty-first century and you guys are nuts." "So this is it, then," she said flatly. "You're saying good-bye."

"This is *not* good-bye, Sparrow. At least not from me. I've been calling home nonstop trying to change their minds. I think Ma's close to admitting that they made a bad move, but Baba's still worried sick, and she won't even let me talk to him."

"So what are you going to do?"

"I'm going home next weekend to convince them that they're wrong. The whole thing's crazy, anyway. What I really want to do is have an honest conversation with Dadu. I mean *you* had nothing to do with stealing the family jute farm—why should *you* be on his blacklist?"

Some of my ancestors might have been involved, Sameera thought. "Do they . . . does he . . . expect your parents to arrange your marriage, too?" she asked hesitantly.

"You mean pick out a wife for me? Er . . . yes." His voice was so low now she could hardly hear it. "I know it sounds crazy for an eighteen-year-old guy to say that he's never had a girlfriend or even gone on a date, but it's true, Sparrow. You're the first girl that ever made me want to—" He stopped.

She leaned closer, and lowered her voice, too. "To what, Bobby?"

He reached for her hand, pulled it across the table, and kissed it. "To break the rules," he said.

The kiss was quick and light, but she could still feel it on her skin when he let go. Sameera wondered if all the clientele inside the Revolutionary Café could feel the heat of it.

"I've never had a boyfriend or dated anyone before either, Bobby," she said. "Crushes, of course, but nothing serious. Until you came along."

"I was pretty sure how you felt that day in the airport, when you looked at me . . ."

"You mean before we got attacked by the pack of Girl Scouts?"

He grinned. "Yeah. Before they descended. Listen,

Sparrow, I'm so sorry I haven't been able to call you. I'm going to figure out a way for this to work, but in the meantime I have to keep my word—I won't lie to my parents."

"What happens if you can't convince them?"

"I'm not coming back to D.C. until I do. I bought my ticket to Charleston already—I leave a week from today," he said.

"I hope they understand, Bobby. I've been missing you so much."

"Me too, Sparrow. Thanks for taking a risk and coming here. For listening. For understanding. It's going to work out, I promise. I have to go now—I'm tutoring in the writing lab and I've got an appointment."

"Okay, Bobby. Let me know what happens."

"I'll call as soon as they change their minds." He stood up, leaned over, kissed her again, this time on the cheek through her veil, and walked out the door.

chapter 8

Sameera sat in a daze, feeling like her internal temperature had just spiked to 104 degrees. So many emotions were roiling inside of her, she hardly noticed when the rest of the SARSA club members rejoined her.

Nadia plopped down in Bobby's seat. "So did he give you

that spiel about his parents being old-fashioned? *I* think he uses the family unit as an excuse to get out of relationships. He's so charming; he hates to be the bad guy and cause any pain."

Her voice had an icy been-there-felt-that edge to it that made Sameera's fever plummet. Information from a rejected girlfriend wannabe wasn't something she could trust. Or was it? Was the stuff about his parents a line? Had he kissed Nadia, too?

But Sangi set things straight right away: "His parents *are* megastrict, Nadia. Unlike yours. Besides, you two were never a couple. Bobby really likes Sameera, and you know it."

Nadia shrugged. "I'm a bit too hot for him to handle, I think. He needs someone sweet and old-fashioned like you, Sparrow. I hope it works out for you guys. If you need a friend to lean on, give me a call."

Sameera's girl hackles rose at the condescension. Besides, the only friend she wanted to talk this whole thing over with was her cousin. Pulling up the sleeve of her burka, she glanced at her watch. "Oh no! I'm going to have to run!"

"Okay, Sparrow," said Sangi. "Thanks for coming."

"You guys will have to visit me at the White House. I want you to meet my cousin. Why don't you plan on having your SARSA meeting there next Friday night?"

"Ooooooh! I'd *love* that!" Nadia's air of superiority vanished; she sounded as excited as one of the airport Girl Scouts.

"That would be amazing, Sparrow," Sangi said.

"Can I bring my Speedo and do laps in the pool?" That was George, of course.

"You can, but you might freeze a body part or two. The pool's outdoors. They built a press room over the indoor one during the Nixon years. I'll call you, Sangi, and set it up. Don't say anything to anybody about my visit, okay?"

"Of course not," said Sangi. "We're Team Sameera, remember?"

It was dark when Sameera made it back to the spa. She'd stuck a piece of folded paper into the back door to wedge it open before she left, and she got back into the locker room just as her cousin emerged from the treatment room.

"That was the most unrelaxing experience of my life," said Miranda, wrapping her lime-and-salt-smelling arms around her cousin. "I'm so glad to see you, Sparrow. I was imagining all kinds of horrible things."

"Ran! I'm in love!"

"You are? So it was worth it, after all."

"Yes, but we can't see each other."

"What? Why not?"

"It's a long story, Ran."

"Well, take your locator back right now, get out of that burka before the Cougars catch you, and let's go straight home so you can tell me everything."

Once they were safely back inside the Residence, Sameera recounted what Bobby had said and done, not everything, but almost everything. She skipped over the kiss part—*that* still felt too tender and private even to share with Ran.

Her cousin was sitting cross-legged on a chair and Sameera was sprawled on her bed, her head resting on Jingle's flank. Both girls were in their red-white-and-blue jammies again. "Wait, let me figure this out," Miranda said. "He likes you, right?"

"*Yes*! Isn't that incredible?"

"Not to me, Sparrow. I know *you*, remember? He'd be nuts not to fall for you. But I don't get it. He didn't call because his *parents* told him not to? How old is this guy again?"

"Eighteen. But it's really important for him to respect his mom and dad."

Her cousin shook her head doubtfully. "I don't want you to get involved with a Peter Panner, Sparrow."

"What's a Peter Panner?" For some reason she felt defensive—she'd expected Miranda to champion Bobby, not criticize him.

"You know—a guy that's stuck permanently in childhood," Miranda said. "Thirty-something dudes still living with their parents?"

"Bobby's not like that, Ran." *Although some Indian thirty-somethings do still live with their parents,* she thought. *And what's wrong with that?*

"Well, what's up with this big Hindi-Muslim divide, then? I hate to say this, Sparrow, but are you sure it's not the world's hugest excuse to avoid a relationship?"

When Nadia had said basically the same thing, doubts had swarmed into Sameera's mind like a horde of small, yipping dogs. Did her cousin really have to rile them up again? Couldn't *anyone* focus on the amazing news that the guy she liked felt the same way about her?

"It's Hind-oo, not Hind-ee," she said. "The first is a religion; the second's a language."

Her cousin looked miffed. "I'm just a *farm girl* from *Ohio*. What do *I* know about *world cultures?*"

Sameera immediately felt bad. "Sorry. I didn't mean to sound like I was talking down to you. It's just that . . . well, if you could have heard how sincere he sounded, and how sweet. He *likes* me, Ran. Isn't that incredible?"

Miranda got over hurt feelings in record time—that was one of the many things Sameera loved about her. "It is, Sparrow. And I'm thrilled for you. At least one of us has a shot at romance this year."

"Yeah. The shortest romance on the planet. We got together and were thwarted in a span of five minutes. Now I've got to wait a whole week until we talk again. That is, *if* he's able to convince them that we can see each other."

"It's going to work out, Sparrow. Besides, this gives you a chance to pick your three nonnegotiables. You were supposed to settle that last summer."

"Oh, yeah. What are yours again?" Sameera asked, even though she already knew the answer.

Her cousin didn't hesitate. "The Three *F*s. And don't

pretend you don't know what they are. My list hasn't changed since I was thirteen."

The ability to have *fun*, a strong *faith*, and unwavering loyalty to *family*. That's what Miranda was looking for in a guy, and she hadn't found it yet—at least not in Maryfield, Ohio.

"Oh yeah, farming, farming, and farming," Sameera said. "Or is it fame, fortune, and Ferraris?"

Miranda ignored her cousin's weak attempt at humor. "You've got to pick three things you can't live without. *Then* you find a guy who has them and ignore most of the stuff he does that drives you nuts."

"Relationships by Ran. What makes you such an expert?"

"I hate to admit it, but I learned from watching my parents," Miranda answered. "Dad's got that annoying habit of sulking when he's mad, and when Mom has a tantrum, there's no stopping her. She gets passionate about politics and hates that he's so calm and rational. But they have the same sense of humor, work well together, and never lie to each other, so they just bear with the irritating stuff and keep going."

Sameera thought about her own parents. They, too, seemed blind to some of the most annoying things about each other. "So that's how you decide if a guy's right for you? Decide which set of bad qualities you want to put up with and ignore the rest?"

"No. You decide what you really treasure and focus on that. It's like that poem Westfield assigned the other day, you know, the one by what's her name. Wait, I'll go get it." Miranda ran to her room and returned with an anthology of women poets.

"It's called 'Appraisal' by Sara Teasdale. Listen, Sparrow." Miranda, using her best theater voice, recited the poem:

> *Never think she loves him wholly,*
> *Never believe her love is blind,*
> *All his faults are locked securely*
> *In a closet of her mind;*
> *All his indecisions folded*
> *Like old flags that time has faded,*
> *Limp and streaked with rain,*
> *And his cautiousness like garments*
> *Frayed and thin, with many a stain—*
> *Let them be, oh let them be,*
> *There is treasure to outweigh them,*
> *His proud will that sharply stirred,*
> *Climbs as surely as the tide,*
> *Senses strained too taut to sleep,*
> *Gentleness to beast and bird,*
> *Humor flickering hushed and wide*
> *As the moon on moving water,*
> *And a tenderness too deep*
> *To be gathered in a word.*

Sameera listened, absentmindedly pulling off strands of Jingle's hair that were brocading her bedcover. She'd always enjoyed her cousin's rich, low reading voice. "So you lock his faults securely in your mind *after* you find the treasures," she said when Miranda was done. "But how do you decide what the treasures *are*?"

"I know what two of yours are already, Sparrow. Just by listening to you talk about Bobby."

"You do?"

"Uh-huh. You're looking for honesty. And courage."

Sameera hesitated, thought it over, and then nodded. "That's true. But what's number three?"

"I don't know. You've got to fill in that blank yourself."

Sameera stayed awake for a long time after her cousin left, thinking about their conversation and the poem. But her last thought before she fell asleep wasn't about Sara Teasdale. It was the recollection of a hand reaching for hers across a coffee table, and the memory of a soft kiss on her skin.

chapter 9

The First Cousin spent most of Saturday morning upstairs in the solarium trying to eke out a tan before the Viennese Ball that night. The pale sunlight that streamed in through the windows wasn't working very well to darken her skin.

Sameera was gazing out at the wintry view as she sprawled on a chaise longue, still thinking about Bobby. She had a sudden urge to watch a favorite classic where the hero and heroine were separated by ancient enmities. *West Side Story*, she thought. *Romeo and Juliet.* Unfortunately, none of them had happy endings. Sameera was hoping that she and Bobby would be the exception that proved the rule. Or better yet, shattered it.

"Do you think I've gotten any color at all, Sparrow?" Miranda asked, putting down the interior design magazine she was reading.

Sameera held her forearm against her cousin's. "I don't get it," she said. "People in India and Pakistan spend bundles on lotions and creams to lighten their skin. Meanwhile, white people in America spend a fortune to get dark."

"In case you haven't noticed, I happen to be a white person in America," Miranda said. "And I just can't be this white if I'm going to look good in that dress tonight. I'll have to use a bronzing lotion."

The door flew open. The girls looked up to see Elizabeth Campbell Righton dressed in bike pants and a sports bra. For once, the First Lady's face wasn't hidden under layers of makeup, and Sameera thought she looked much younger than she did on television.

"Ready for our workout, Sparrow?"

Sameera jumped up. She'd forgotten that she and her mother had planned to start their Manuel: He Moves You

White House routine this morning. Good thing she was already wearing yoga pants and tennis shoes.

"How was the spa?" Mom asked.

"Fine," answered Miranda quickly.

"Er . . . okay." Sameera hated to keep secrets from her parents, mainly because they'd always trusted her so much. But putting on a burka had been the only way to talk to Bobby without Cougars and Rhinos in tow. She'd tell Mom and Dad about her adventure soon, once a bit more time had passed. Besides, she wasn't planning on using her disguise again. At least she didn't think so.

"So . . . how's it going as First Lady, Aunt Liz?" Miranda asked.

"I'm loving it. I've got the biggest platform on Earth to fight for my refugees, and everybody's got to listen. I'm supposed to find an American issue, too, but that shouldn't be too hard. How were your first sessions with Westfield, Miranda?"

"She's great," Miranda answered. "I love the fact that it's only a two-hour school day. Leaves me with lots of time to do other stuff."

"Like what?" Mom asked.

"Oh, memorize lines from movie scripts. You know, just in case I get my big chance while I'm here. I plan on heading back with a get-out-of-dairy-farming-forever card in my pocket, you know."

Hmmmm, Sameera thought. *I never see her memorizing lines. All I see her doing is using that camera. A lot.*

"What about college?" Mom asked. "You've only got one more year at Maryfield High. Doesn't graduating count as a way to leave the farm?"

"Nope. Four years of college just delays your re-entry. The only one who's ever escaped the cows forever is you, Aunt Liz. I can't believe *my* mother actually chose the life by marrying Dad."

Elizabeth Campbell Righton frowned, and Sameera knew she was tempted to deliver the family's four-point "dairy farming is a noble profession" lecture. *Miranda knows it by heart, Mom,* Sameera thought. *Don't go there. She's got to figure things out herself.*

This time, Mom made the right choice. "Your mother's been trying to call your cell for the last two days," she said. "Why aren't you picking up?"

"I turned it off," Miranda said. "My phone bill's gotten way out of control."

Sameera and Mom avoided eye contact. Before Miranda joined them in the White House, they'd brainstormed how to handle the sticky financial issue, but nothing resembling a decent plan had emerged.

"Miranda, you've given up a lot to come out here and be Sameera's companion," Mom ventured cautiously now. "Why not accept an allowance from your Uncle James and me? We'd be so happy if you did."

Miranda leaped up. "You want to *pay* me to spend time with my *cousin*?" she demanded. "You're going to give me an *allowance* to live in this amazing place? That's terrible,

Aunt Liz. I've got the same Campbell pride you do, don't forget."

"Okay, okay. Settle down. But most seventeen-year-olds who *aren't* living in the White House could find a part-time job somewhere. Tell you what—I'll ask around to see if anybody inside the place needs some paid help."

Miranda sat down again. "You will? Aunt Liz, that would be fantastic. Maybe I could help out in the kitchen—I'm a good cook, you know that."

"Don't get your hopes up, Ran," Sameera warned. "The Pandas seem sort of territorial when it comes to their kitchen."

"We'll see what happens," Mom said. "Here, take my phone and give your parents a call."

Sameera followed her mother to the gym across the hall and climbed on the treadmill, punching in some settings to get the thing going. Beside her, Mom was pressing buttons on the elliptical machine, and they started moving at exactly the same time.

"Mom, do you know anything about my relatives?" Sameera asked, adjusting the incline so it felt like she was climbing a steep hill. "They were Muslims, right?"

Elizabeth Campbell Righton glanced quickly at her daughter. "Yes, darling. But you know that already. Is there any reason it's coming up again? Are people leaving mean comments on your blog?"

"Actually, it's working the other way. Sparrowbloggers are getting to know each other and sending notes to other

Sparrowbloggers instead of just to me. Any newbie who sounds the least bit mean is straightened out pretty quickly by the regulars. It's getting to be a safe place, but people still have the freedom to say what they think, which I like."

Like Sparrowhawk, she thought. Other commenters had responded to the "privileged white girl in camo" accusation, but Sameera knew she was going to have to say something, too. She just didn't know what yet.

"That's because of you, Sparrow," Mom said, increasing the pace of her machine. "You've got this way of making people feel welcome, like they can ask anything and you'll always tell the truth."

Again, that twinge of guilt. "So, Mom. Are you one hundred percent sure that I'm a Muslim?"

Beads of moisture were already forming on the First Lady's forehead. "I've always said that your faith journey's up to you, Sparrow. I can't force you to believe in—"

"Maybe that wasn't the right question. I don't mean what I *believe*, Mom. I mean what I *am*. By blood. Or DNA." Sameera went back to a zero decline on her treadmill.

Mom kept talking, even though she was getting out of breath. "Well, as you know, darling," she panted, "we've always assumed . . . you were from a Muslim . . . family . . . because that part of Pakistan . . . where the orphanage was . . . is almost all Muslim."

So that was that then. Sameera pictured a horde of her ancestors clutching burning torches as they stormed across the border into Bobby's village.

Mom pressed the pause button on her elliptical, took a big swig of water, and mopped her face with a towel. "I'm out of shape again, darn it. Must have been all that chocolate I ate in Maryfield. Manuel's eyes got huge when he saw me; he made me promise to do a half hour of cardio every day this week." She climbed back on the machine and started it again, setting it this time at a much slower pace. "You think Ran's doing okay, Sparrow? Was it a good idea to bring her here?"

"It's great, except that she's so prickly about money," Sameera answered.

"I know. But wouldn't you be if you were in her shoes?"

"I guess."

"Miranda's only staying until June, Sparrow, and then you're going to need some friends. Maybe we could invite a few flesh-and-blood Sparrowbloggers who live around here to come over sometime."

"I've been thinking about that, Mom. Remember Mariam, the girl I met when I . . . went shopping on my own last August?"

"Of course I do. Yes, she'd be perfect. She lives in D.C., right?"

Sameera managed to take a swig of water without slowing her treadmill. "Yeah, well, I'm thinking of inviting her over. And then there's my SARSA buddies at G-Dub."

"Right. Sangita. Nadia. George. And Bobby, of course. Have you heard much from him? I really liked him, even though we didn't get much of a chance to talk that day."

"You mean the day you asked him to turn from evil and repent?"

Mom grinned. "I was a bit over the top, wasn't I? I felt horrible about that. I'm so sorry, Sameera."

"It's okay, Mom. You were tired. He understood."

"I've been dying to ask about him, but the parenting books tell you to 'let your teenager take the lead' when it comes to conversations about relationships. Your grandmother, of course, told me to jump right in. 'They want to tell you,' she said. 'They just don't know how.'"

"You told Gran about Bobby?"

"I didn't have to. When you opened that gorgeous photo, Sparrow, my love, it didn't take a rocket scientist to figure out how you're feeling about this guy. Well? It seemed like things were starting to simmer between the two of you, but maybe I'm just imagining things."

Part of Sameera suddenly wanted to confess everything that had happened the night before. *I'm in love, Mom. But we can't be together. And I ditched the Secret Service without them even realizing it.* She wasn't sure she could keep the last bit a secret much longer, *or* the first—especially from her mother. But this didn't feel like the right time, with sweat dripping from both of them, and her mother starting to pant again. Not to mention having to explain everything twice because her father wasn't around. Repeating the same conversation was a liability of having busy parents.

She stopped her treadmill. "He's a good guy," she said. "Time for my weights."

"Not for me," Mom said, increasing her pace again. "I've still got twenty minutes to go. How much chocolate did I eat, anyway? And why didn't you people stop me?"

Sameera picked up a pair of ten-pound free weights and started the bicep curls Manuel had put on her training agenda. "You get sort of . . . tense . . . when somebody moderates your sugar intake, Mom. Dad and I learned the hard way that it's better not to say anything."

"Enablers. Both of you."

Sameera grinned. "Gran sure had a few things to say about you staying in your pajamas all day and eating chocolate."

"Yep. Made me run . . . to store . . . buy three more bars . . . can't talk . . . any more. About to die."

chapter 10

The five-member color team came down the Grand Staircase, carrying the American and presidential flags. Sameera counted them off as she waited on the landing: Army, Navy, Marines, Air Force, Coast Guard. Mom and Dad followed them into the room as the Marine band began playing the fanfare, "Ruffles and Flourishes," and then shifted into "Hail to the Chief." *Some traditions are keepers,* Sameera thought, humming a joyful accompaniment.

With Peter and Miranda right behind Wilhelm and Sameera, six couples sauntered arm in arm down the Grand Staircase, through the Cross Hall, and into the East Room. A host of bejeweled, tuxedoed, and designer-gowned guests made appreciative noises as they entered. Matching her steps to Wilhelm's, Sameera concentrated fiercely on the intricacies of the opening choreography she and Ran had learned in such a short time. There, it was done, and perfectly, too. The cousins exchanged grins that had to substitute for their signature triumphant fist punch.

The music picked up for the less-complicated Viennese waltz part of the dance, and Wilhelm started spinning Sameera around the room. She felt like she was floating, and with each song, found herself enjoying the whirling, swirling rhythm more and more. *If only I were dancing with Bobby,* Sameera thought, as her partner's strong hand steered her safely around the room. *Bhangra or ballroom, it doesn't matter as long as he's the one holding me.*

They danced over to her cousin, who was excusing herself from Peter and looking extremely pale despite the bronzing lotion she'd slathered across every inch of exposed skin. A middle-aged, balding guest was ogling Miranda's halter dress, and Sameera placed herself strategically to block his view. "You okay, Ran?" she asked.

"I never liked that teacups ride much either," Miranda said ruefully. "I'm going to run upstairs for a minute until I stop feeling dizzy. I'll be right back."

Sameera returned to spinning around the room, this time with Peter leading her. She waltzed by Tara, who was sitting at a table by herself. As usual, the First Lady's right-hand woman was beautifully dressed, but Sameera noticed she was scribbling notes with a stylus onto a handheld. *Tara definitely needs a life,* Sameera thought.

At the head table, President James Righton looked elegant and confident in his tuxedo, his usual diplomatic courtesy intact as he conversed with each person who approached him. Sameera, however, could tell he was bored stiff. She noticed one shiny patent-leather-encased presidential foot tapping under the table in time to the music. Her father loved to dance as much as she did.

When the orchestra segued into the slower one-two-three beat of a familiar Strauss waltz, Sameera excused herself from Peter and made her way to the head table. An Austrian official was droning on about some trade issue that he obviously cared about a great deal. "Dad," Sameera said, interrupting the conversation. "Dance with me."

President James Righton leaped to his feet. "Will you excuse me?" he asked his dinner companion. "When your daughter asks for a dance, it's an opportunity you don't want to miss."

Sameera heard the minister laughing indulgently behind them as she put her hand into the crook of her father's elbow and walked out to the dance floor. They'd danced together since she was a little girl, and the music quickly pulled them into a familiar, easygoing circle of two.

"Thanks, Sparrow," Dad said in a low voice. "That dude was amazingly dull. A one-man miracle cure for insomnia. What's up with you?"

"We're having a family dinner tomorrow night, Dad," Sameera informed him. "I want to talk about something important."

"Sounds more interesting than tonight's conversations, that's for sure. Can you give me a preview?"

"Er . . . not now, Dad. Don't want Mom to feel out of the loop, right? I'll wait until it's just the four of us."

"Scotchies for dessert, I hope?"

"I'll see if Ran can whip some up after church."

"With that amazing frosting she makes?"

"Definitely."

"Where *is* Miranda, anyway?" Dad asked, his eyes scanning the room over Sameera's shoulder as they turned to the music.

Sameera glanced around, too. Her cousin was still nowhere in sight. "Maybe I should—"

"There she is," Dad said, his voice sounding relieved. "She certainly loves that camera, doesn't she?"

Another half turn and Sameera caught sight of her cousin filming the scene. "Yeah. I haven't seen any of her footage yet. She must have hours of it by now."

"That camera's almost as good as a burka, isn't it?" Dad asked.

"What?" Sameera tried not to reveal her surprise at her father's choice of analogy.

"It hides a lot of Miranda's face," Dad said. "Reminds me of that head covering you used last fall as a getaway costume. The best part is that people can't tell if she's zooming in on them or on something else."

They turned again and Sameera saw Miranda aim the camera directly at the balding guy who'd been leering at her earlier. The man blushed, stumbled, and steered his partner in the opposite direction. "You know, I think you're right, Dad. It sort of . . . puts her in charge of who's being watched, doesn't it?"

Dad and Sameera danced a few more songs, lapsing into a comfortable, pressure-free silence. Before long, though, Mom tottered over and tapped Sameera's shoulder. "I'm cutting in," she said. "And James, don't talk or expect me to say anything. I'm exhausted. Just hold me up and pretend you're having fun."

"But I am, darling," Dad said as he smiled at Sameera and whirled Mom away.

Sameera went off in search of Miranda. She found her cousin in the kitchen filming the head pastry chef as he prepared a dessert that flamed and reeked of alcohol.

"Just a minute, Sparrow," Miranda muttered. "They're almost done."

Suddenly, the camera shut itself off with a complaining whir followed by a decisive click. "Did you get it, Miss Campbell?" the pastry chef asked eagerly.

"Sorry, Mr. Phillips. I'm out of memory."

He looked disappointed. "Come back on Monday," he

said. "Your aunt's first official tea is coming up, and I've got some exciting *petits fours* that I want to practice making. Now *that* should be great on film."

Miranda smiled, but she shook her head. "No can do, Mr. Phillips. We'll have to wait for another opportunity."

The girls walked out of the kitchen and back into the East Room. "Are you busy on Monday, Ran?" Sameera asked. "It might be good to get those Pandas on your side, especially if you want to work with them."

"No. I'm out of memory, Sparrow. Didn't you hear me the first time?"

"Get some more, then," Sameera said, without thinking.

Miranda didn't reply, but Sameera could read her mind: *It costs money.* "Download your footage onto a computer, clear out the memory card, and start again," she suggested. "Anyway, maybe this is a sign that you should start editing what you've already got instead of filming new stuff all the time."

Miranda chewed her lower lip.

"What's wrong now?" Sameera asked.

"I don't have the software I need to make the kind of movies I want to make," Miranda confessed. "*Why* did I spend all my money on this dress, Sparrow? Next time, grab my wallet and run. Fast."

"Use my laptop, Ran," Sameera said quickly. "It came with some fancy moviemaking software that I've never used—you could use it to edit your footage, add music, make it into what you want it to be. I could even post some of your clips on my blog if you want."

"Slow down, Sparrow. Why can't I use your software on the White House PCs?"

"Because my system's not compatible with the White House machines. Besides, mine's five times faster than the ones they have sitting around here, and easier to use, too."

"But you're on your computer all the time. It's, like, your most personal item. Are you sure you want to share it?"

Sameera locked her laptop case every night to guarantee that only she had access to her personal information. Not that the impeccably honest staff in the White House would steal anything, of course, but there was something about shielding her precious possession from strange eyes that gave her a sense of security. But this wasn't a stranger—this was Miranda, beloved cousin and best friend. "I'll share it with you," Sameera said, trying not to sound in the least bit reluctant. *Too bad we didn't get her some moviemaking software along with that camera,* she thought.

The orchestra was taking a break, and Sameera noticed her parents had been commandeered by the one-man insomnia cure again. Mom was propping her chin on both fists to prevent her head from flopping forward. Dad was nodding, looking fascinated while the guy droned on.

"Come on, Ran," Sparrow said as the orchestra started up again. "Wilhelm's waving at me. I'll dance with him; you go rescue my father."

chapter 11

When the Rightons took their seats in a balcony pew on Sunday morning, Sameera glimpsed both Mature Cougar and Young Cougar standing at the rear of the church and felt another twinge of guilt. Her little trip to the Revolutionary Café could have gotten the agents into serious trouble. She'd have to make it up to them somehow, even though they didn't know how close they'd come to getting fired because of her.

As the service progressed, Sameera listened to the sermon and stood and sat down at the right times, but she couldn't stop thinking about Bobby. She reached for one of the prayer request cards in the rack in front of her and filled it out: "Please pray for Bobby Ghosh's grandfather, who is very ill." *Pray for Bobby Ghosh, too,* she added silently, dropping the card into the offering basket. *And me, while you're at it.*

Finally, everyone stood up to sing the doxology, and the minister raised his hands to offer the benediction. Sameera followed her parents down the stairs and outside to a sidewalk jammed with tourists and gawkers. Miranda immediately whipped out her camera and started filming; she'd stayed up late the night before downloading her footage onto Sameera's laptop to clear her memory card.

It was a mostly friendly crowd, with people smiling, waving, and wanting to shake hands. Then, out of nowhere, a voice boomed out: "Hey, Paki! Go back to Pakistan!"

Sameera was squeezing the outstretched hands of three ancient, beaming women. *Great,* she thought. *A heckler.* Just what she needed. *Ignore it,* she warned herself sternly, just as she learned to do during the campaign. *Don't respond.* She noticed her mother's head swiveling as Elizabeth Campbell Righton tried to identify the shouter. Secret Service agents hustled the First Family along, and Dad smiled and waved before climbing into Cadillac One, his face calm as though he hadn't heard a thing.

"Muslim Lover!" It was Angry Voice again.

That was it. The First Lady stopped like a NASCAR driver slamming on the brakes. She turned to face the direction where the person with the voice was hiding. "Exactly *who* are you talking about?" she called. "President Righton? Me? Or *Jesus Himself*?"

Good one, Mom, Sameera thought, staying right by her mother and wishing she could whip out a notepad to take notes. This incident was definitely blogworthy; she was already curious about Sparrowhawk's take on it.

The crowd was booing the heckler and calling out, "Go, Mrs. Righton!" Sameera's row of ancient women were practically growling as they expressed their feelings toward him.

Miranda kept filming. She wasn't budging either.

"Follow your husband into the car, ma'am," pleaded an agent.

"Let's go, Peanut," commanded a voice in Sameera's ear. "Come on, Peach."

It was Young Cougar, steering them gently but firmly into the armored limo. Even inside the car, Miranda stayed glued to her camera, cracking the window to poke the lens out. She stopped filming only when the crowd was no longer in sight.

"Thanks for sticking up for me, sweetheart," James Righton told his wife. "But idiots like that come with the territory. We're open game now, remember?"

"I don't care," Mom said, obviously still steaming. "Once you're the First Lady, you lose the right to get mad? And any passing idiot can yell something like that and get away with it?"

"Freedom of speech, Mom," Sameera said. "This is America."

"Stars learn to handle it, Auntie Liz," Miranda added. "I've seen actors return nasty comments with a smile and a wave."

Elizabeth Campbell Righton shook her head. "That sounds too wimpy to me."

Sameera grinned. "Turn the other cheek, Mom. You're the one who always brings up Jesus."

"I suppose you're right," Mom relented, sighing. "I can't respond to every jerk on the planet by turning into a jerk myself. I'm kind of burned out, I guess."

"What you need is a quiet dinner at home, just the four of us," Sameera said.

"That sounds fabulous, Sparrow."

Dad leaned over and kissed his wife on the neck. "First comes an afternoon for just the two of us."

The cousins groaned.

"Too much information, Dad," Sameera said.

"Wait till you're alone, Uncle James," pleaded Miranda.

"Oh, we plan to," said Dad.

Judging by the grin on her face, Elizabeth Campbell Righton was looking forward to the afternoon as much as her husband was.

chapter 12

While the president and First Lady had some time to themselves, Miranda and Sameera wandered down to the big kitchen on the first floor. They were hoping to borrow the ingredients needed to bake frosted oatmeal scotchies for dessert.

Mr. Phillips smiled when Miranda told him what she was making. "Those are exactly the kind of cookies my grandmother used to make," he said. "I've been hunting for a good recipe, but nothing out there seems right. Do you think I could have a sample when they're done?"

"Of course," Miranda said. "I'll bring down a plate."

Sameera left her cousin humming, baking, and mixing in the family kitchen and headed for the Lincoln Sitting Room. She sat on one of the wing chairs and opened her laptop, relishing the strange sensation of homecoming that she always got when she powered up. It was time to compose a new entry on her blog.

> I have a question for you, intergalactics. Don't get me wrong, I love my life, and I'm certainly not whining about going to parties and getting to meet famous people. But as my Gran always put it, "to whom much has been given, much will be required," so I'm trying to figure out what's required of ME during these four years. Of course, having fun is a perfectly decent thing to do, but is it enough? That's why I thought I'd ask if you want to read about fun stuff or have me feature more serious posts on Sparrowblog. All votes greatly appreciated. Remember, keep those comments short, clean, and to the point. Peace be with you. Sparrow.

Next, it was time to answer Mariam's e-mail:

> Hey, Mariam! So great to hear from you. I'm thinking of having a get-together on Friday with some friends of mine from George

Washington University. Do you want to join us?
I'd like you to meet my cousin, too. We'll
probably just have pizza—no pepperoni or any
other pork, I promise. Tell your parents, too,
that although one boy might be here with us,
the whole evening will be chaperoned by a
grown-up at all times. (Thanks to the Secret
Service. They come in handy sometimes.) If
you can make it, send a note, and I'll
dispatch a car to pick you up.

Much love to you, your parents, and your
grandmother from your friend Sameera.

She powered down when Miranda came to find her, and
they walked back across the hall to set the round table in
the family dining room. "I posted on my blog today, but
I'm wondering if we shouldn't stick to the Maryfield 'no-
screens-or-plugs-on-Sunday' rule from now on," she told
Ran, who was filling the water glasses. "It's sort of relaxing to detox from the Web one day a week."

"Fine. I've gotten used to that rule after all these years,
and I actually like it—don't tell Poppa that. But drop the
holy act, Sparrow. I know why you don't feel the need to
get online every five minutes. It's because you know Bobby
can't send you anything."

Sameera, who had just lit the tall, tapered candles on
the table, sighed so heavily that she extinguished one of

them. "I sure hope that conversation with his parents goes well. I should have told him about my make-your-parents-see-the-light family dinner plan."

"Is that what we're doing? Are you going to tell your parents about Bobby?"

"No. I don't have to ask them for permission when it comes to dating. At least, I don't think so. We're definitely not as old-fashioned as Bobby's family."

"Hey, your Hollywood heroes in black-and-white fantasyland are all old-fashioned. Humphrey Bogart. *Casablanca*. Cary Grant. *An Affair to Remember*. Gregory Peck. *Roman Holiday*."

Sameera grinned. Her cousin had named three of the movies they'd watched yet again over the holidays—mostly for the sake of the brilliant and beautiful heroes who lit up the screen. "Bogart. Now there's a hero for you. Sacrificing hope of future happiness for his lady love . . . and the greater good."

"Well, Bobby made a sacrifice, didn't he? It must have been humiliating to admit he thinks it's important to obey his parents. Telling the truth like that took courage, so that proves he's got two out of your three treasures."

Sameera glanced at her reflection on a knife before setting it on the table. "Yeah, he's definitely honest, even with his parents. Meanwhile, here I am, sneaking around behind *my* parents' backs."

"Oh, so that's what this dinner is about—your illegal trip to that coffeehouse. Well, they didn't freak out the last time they found out about your getaway disguise, right?"

"Yeah, but that's not on the agenda. I'm not sure they're going to be as quick to forgive this time. The stakes are a lot higher now that I'm First Daughter."

"You're right. Don't confess tonight. They need to relax. So what are we trying to get them to see the light about?"

"Ran, what do you think about me enrolling in school next year?"

Miranda raised her eyebrows. "You mean here in D.C.? What about Westfield?"

"I already talked to her about it. She thinks it's a great idea. I want to mention it tonight and see how my parents take it."

Jean-Claude was at the door, wheeling in the dinner the girls had ordered. "Here you go, ladies. A country-style Sunday steak-and-baked-potato dinner for four. Everything's hot and steaming, so gather your parents."

"You get them, Sparrow," Ran said. "I don't want to interrupt anything."

"What? I'm their kid. It's way more embarrassing for me."

They ended up doing rock, paper, scissors to see who had to summon Sameera's parents, and Miranda lost. While she was gone, Sameera lifted the stainless steel domes on the serving cart. The baked potatoes were crisped to perfection and came with sour cream, chives, and fresh bacon bits. Chilled forks and salad plates were included for the Cobb salad the girls had ordered. There was only one thing missing, and a quick intercom buzz brought Jean-Claude racing back up with a bottle of steak sauce. *There,* Sameera thought. *NOW everything's ready.*

Mom arrived in jeans and an old blouse without a trace of makeup and her hair stuffed into a ponytail. Dad was wearing the fleecy Ohio State sweatshirt and sweatpants that Poppa and Gran had given him for Christmas. He had a trendy-looking afternoon shadow on his chin and cheeks.

Sameera served the food as the family gathered around the table. "So what's the purpose of this family dinner, girls?" Dad asked, filling two goblets with the red wine that had been sent up for him and Mom. The girls were drinking milk, of course.

"Come on, Dad, aren't you tired of agendas?" Sameera asked. "Let the conversation flow for a change. Eat. Drink. Relax." Her father was too savvy for her own good.

Dad took a sip of wine. "You're right, Sparrow. Mmm. This vino is dee-vy-no. I think we should be strict about taking a day of rest while we're in the White House, Liz. Let's avoid scheduling anything on Sunday evenings unless a dire emergency comes up."

The food was savored, the wine sipped, the milk chugged, and Dad's bad puns inspired even more tacky ones around the table. "Actually, there is something I want to talk about," Sameera said, as Ran passed around her oven-warm, frosted scotchies.

"Sounds ominous," said Dad.

"It's not. Mom, Dad, I'm wondering if I should enroll in school next fall."

"School? But why would you want to do that? Don't you like Westfield?" Mom asked.

"She's great, but I'd like to be involved in extracurricu-lars again, like journalism and sports."

James Righton was frowning. "What about security is-sues? Times have changed since the last president had a school-aged child. And besides, Sparrow, your practice SAT scores in math are better, but Westfield needs more time to work her miracles. A private tutor could bring you up to speed for college much faster than a school."

"We can work out the security stuff, Dad. And West-field could keep tutoring me after school."

"This place could get kinda lonely for Sparrow after I leave," Miranda added.

"Now that's a good point," Mom said.

"And we don't have to decide now," Sameera said quickly. "We can mull it over for a while and gather some informa-tion—maybe visit some of the schools that have educated First Daughters in the past to find out how they handle security."

Her parents looked at each other. Dad shrugged. Mom nodded. "Okay, Sparrow," she said. "I'll ask Tara to set something up."

"More scotchies, Dad?" Sameera asked, passing the plate to her father.

"Sure, bribe me," the president said glumly, reaching for two. "I swore I wasn't going to be one of those wimpy fa-thers whose daughters could charm them into saying yes to anything, but it's hard, Sparrow, it's hard."

chapter 13

On Tuesdays, it was Sameera's turn to take the second tutoring session. She labored over geometry with Westfield, but it didn't feel like she was making much progress.

"You got a few more opinions on your fun versus serious post, Sparrow," Miranda called through the open door between the two rooms. She was borrowing Sameera's laptop. Again.

"Sparrow's busy right now, Miranda," said Westfield. She was usually the most patient of tutors, but proofs were completely stumping Sameera and exasperating both of them.

Sameera gazed through the open door longingly at her cousin—and her laptop. "What'd they say, Ran? It's a tie so far. Half my readers want me to be serious and deal with real issues, and the other half want me to bring them into the fun."

"It's still a tie. Sparrowhawk posted again and said that if you don't get serious soon, she's tuning out. But a couple of other readers want a detailed description of the Viennese Ball."

"Sparrow, we've only got about a half hour left," Westfield warned. "Back to work."

Sameera sighed. "Shut down the browser and my mail, Ran. I'm getting tortured. I mean tutored."

"You've got to go the distance, Sparrow," Westfield said, eerily channeling Jacques, Sameera's crew coach back in Brussels. "Your first try at the SATs is only a couple of months away, and then you'll have to take them again in the fall. Have you thought about where you're going to apply to college?"

"Of course," Sameera answered. "Ohio State. Berkeley. Calvin College. Oh, and George Washington University." She ignored the knowing look Ran sent her way. "They've all got great journalism programs. Which reminds me, Westfield, if I'm going to be a reporter, why do I need math?"

"To survive," Westfield grunted. "We've gone over that a hundred times, Sparrow."

Sameera glanced at her watch—only twenty-five minutes left. "What about you, Ran?" she called through the open door, banking on the fact that the tutor would be interested in her cousin's answer. "Which colleges are you thinking about?"

Miranda was trying to figure out the filmmaking software that came with Sameera's turbocharged laptop. She looked up distractedly. "Oh, I'll go to Ohio State eventually, Sparrow, you know that. Everybody in our family does. But I'm going to earn some major money first."

"Why not go straight to college?" Westfield asked. "Ohio State has a great theater program—"

"I'm not interested in paying back college loans." Miranda went back to frowning at the laptop screen.

There's the money thing again, Sameera thought. *Wonder if Mom's made any progress in her find-Ran-a-job mission.*

Westfield tapped Sameera's hand with her pencil. You *say something,* she mouthed.

"Might as well keep all the doors open by going to college first, Ran," Sameera called, trying to rise to the occasion.

"Yes," said Westfield. "Hollywood, college, dairy farming—"

Miranda got up and stormed over to the door. "I am not going to be a dairy farmer or marry a dairy farmer or live anywhere near Merry Dude Dairy Farm!" *Slam!* She prevented the possibility of any further questioning.

"Wow, her voice sounds exactly like Mom's when *she* gets going," Sameera marveled. "I guess that settles it, then. *I'll* take over the farm. I'll care for the cows by day and write my syndicated column by night."

"Or *I'll* take over the farm," Westfield said. "Maybe then I'll be able to figure out how to bake some of those oatmeal scotchies. Mine just don't come out right, and believe me, I've tried."

"The secret's in the frosting, Westfield. Or really, in the milk we use *for* the frosting. Pure fresh Merry Dude Dairy Farm milk."

"Okay, back to work. Quit trying to distract me by talking about food."

Miranda, once again demonstrating the amazing Campbell facility of getting mad and then forgetting about it instantly, reappeared to give their tutor her usual good-bye hug.

"Hey, are you free for dinner tonight, Westfield?" Sameera asked. "Ran and I want to try out that new bistro in Georgetown."

Westfield shook her head. "Sorry, girls, but I'm having dinner at your father's old rival's house. Tommy's got a free night, and Senator Banforth invited me to come and see him."

Senator Victoria Banforth narrowly lost to James Righton in the presidential race, and her son Thomas was studying to be a lawyer at Georgetown. Westfield had tutored him, too, along with many other children on Capitol Hill, including Tara when her father, Senator Sam Colby, served two terms.

"Lucky you," Miranda said. "That Thomas Banforth is luscious . . . and practically our neighbor since he transferred to a D.C. school."

"He *is* a doll, isn't he? A bit young for me, but that's life. And the best part is that he's just as nice on the inside as on the outside. Okay, ladies. See you tomorrow."

"Need your laptop, Sparrow?" Miranda asked, obviously itching to get back to her movie.

"Er . . . no. Not yet, anyway. I need some fresh air for my tired brain," she said quickly. "And so does Jingle."

She let the dog off his leash so he could mark bushes in the Rose Garden, prowl around the winter skeleton of the

Jackson magnolia on the South Lawn, and sniff the roots of several leafless but stately elms. But he was more interested in herding squirrels. *They aren't cows, you silly dog,* Sameera thought, chasing him almost down to the gate before she could get him leashed again. Two Secret Service agents raced after them.

Despite the fact that it was thirty degrees and late on a Tuesday afternoon, tourists and Rhinos alike peered through the wrought-iron gates, lenses poking through to try and catch a shot of any member of the First Family. Sameera waved to the cameras before leading Jingle uphill again. She'd love to talk shop with the reporters on the White House beat, especially the bloggers, to find out how they picked content and handled hypercritical or controlling commenters. But it would be hard to have a candid conversation with a hundred cameras pointing and flashing in your face. Maybe she could visit the White House press room again. She'd passed through it only once, right after her father's first official press conference. It had been full of empty takeout containers and tired-looking people typing on laptops, and she'd felt immediately at home.

Young Cougar was on the detail covering her this afternoon. The other agent was walking farther away, keeping an eye on the crowds lining the gate, but Sameera could see Y. C.'s breath in the frosty air every time she turned. "Come join me!" she called to him, veering away from the gates and heading toward the more secluded Children's Garden.

He walked faster to catch up. "Our K-9 agents have always been labs," he told Sameera as they walked around the pond and stepped over the bronze handprints left behind by other First Children and First Grandchildren. "This dog would have been a good one. He doesn't stray far from your side. Unless he gets tempted by one of those squirrels."

"He misses the farm. He's getting stiff from not running free every day. I hate to say it, but I think Ran should take him when she goes back in June."

"Maybe you can get a puppy," he said. His walkie-talkie beeped, and he spoke into his mouthpiece. "Peanut's in the PP. Peach is in the nest. Where's the Dove? Okay. Ten-four. Over and out."

Was he referring to her having to go to the bathroom? Did these guys know *everything*? Oh, she got it now—PP, short for President's Park, the formal name for the grounds around the White House. "What's your name?" Sameera asked. "I hope it's okay to ask."

"Everybody calls me JB," he said.

"Which stands for . . . ?"

"Jefferson Butler Williams at your service. But nobody's called me that since the second grade."

They walked into the spacious reception hall and shook the snow off their boots. "So where *is* the Dove?" Sameera asked.

"In the East Wing with the Bomb—I mean the Fish—er, I mean, with Miss Colby."

Sameera stopped walking and turned to face him. "Is that her code name, the Fish?"

"Yeah, but I didn't name her that," he said sheepishly. "My suggestion was the Bomb."

"Short for *bombshell*, you mean, or the explosive kind?"

"Well, I was thinking it was short for bombshell, but I didn't tell the guys that. How'd you guess?"

"Intuition. So you think she's attractive, right?"

"Definitely," he admitted. "The other agents think she's a cold fish, but I kind of like her. She's got spine, you know, not like some wishy-washy ladies out there who don't know what they want. She'd make a great agent."

Sameera stole a quick look at his left hand. *Hmmm . . . no ring.* Her own romance was on hold until Bobby's return next week, but there was no reason why she couldn't make things happen for someone else. "Are you on my detail just for the afternoon, JB?" she asked, putting Jingle back on his leash.

"All the way until the late shift, actually."

"Then let's go see what Mom's up to."

chapter 14

Sameera and the agent walked through the long, glassed-in colonnade to the East Wing, which was still bustling with activity even though it was five-thirty in the afternoon. In the sunny, large First Lady's office, Mom, Tara, and a couple of other staffers were sitting around the small oval meeting table. Sameera couldn't see JB's eyes behind his glasses, but she hoped they were taking in the tight-fitting navy suit with white piping that showed off Tara's figure.

"Hi, Sparrow," Mom said. "We're trying to narrow down the choices for my domestic issue. Want to join us for a brainstorming session? I'm thinking illegal immigrants, but these people think that's too controversial."

"Maybe later, Mom. Ran's waiting for me upstairs. Which reminds me—any progress on finding her a job?"

Mom turned to Tara with a questioning look.

Tara shook her head. "Nothing yet. But we're still looking around."

"Good. Did you set up a school visit yet?"

"I've already contacted St. Matthew's," Tara said. "It's the finest private school for girls in the D.C. area—most of the political daughters go there, so you should feel right at home."

"Isn't that where you went?"

"It is indeed. I know the headmistress." She flipped open her handheld and consulted the screen. "We've got an appointment this Thursday."

"Great. Hey, Mom, what are you and Dad doing tonight?"

Another questioning look traveled from Elizabeth Campbell Righton to Tara, who tapped a stylus on the screen of her handheld Master First Lady Planner.

"You have a dinner with a dozen visiting governors, Liz," Tara said. "And their spouses. Seven-thirty sharp."

"Do you have to be there, Tara?" Sameera asked.

Tara looked up, eyes narrowing slightly. "No. Why?"

"I was wondering if you'd like to join Ran and me for dinner in Georgetown tonight. That new bistro got a great review in the paper and we've been wanting to try it. Strictly for fun, of course. No business."

"You should go, Tara," Mom said. "You spend way too much time in the office. You need to have some fun."

Tara seemed surprised. "You really want me to come?" she asked Sameera.

"Of course," said Sameera.

"Okay. I'll meet you in the front hall at seven-forty-five," said Tara, smiling. "I hope what I'm wearing is okay."

"Looks great," said Sameera. "Doesn't it, JB?"

He was still standing in the back of the room, as silent and vigilant as ever. "Yes, ma'am," he answered crisply.

Mom threw Sameera an I-know-you're-up-to-something

look. "Sounds like a plan. Now let's get back to our session. I'm not really interested in censoring the entertainment industry, Tara. I hardly watch any movies, and—"

The door flew open, and in rushed Miranda. She was breathless, flushed, excited. "You'll *never* guess what happened."

"What happened, Ran?"

Miranda threw her arms open and spun around the room in her own partner-free version of the Viennese waltz, reminding Sameera exactly of Julie Andrews in the opening scene of *The Sound of Music.* "Jerry Gaithers wants to meet me," her cousin was caroling instead of "the hills are alive." "Jerry Gaithers. Me. Jerry Gaithers. Me. Jerry. Me."

Sameera was sure that her own face was as blank as her mother's. Tara, however, looked amazed. "Jerry *Gaithers?* Are you sure, Miranda?" she asked.

Miranda stopped spinning and whirling, which was good, because Sameera was getting dizzy watching. And so was Jingle, who was leaping madly around Miranda, offering himself to her as a possible dance partner.

"Yes. Yes. Yes," said Miranda. "I was browsing through Sparrowblog to check in on the conversation. Well, guess what? Someone had *just* posted a comment asking me to contact Gaithers's secretary. I wasn't sure it was legit, but I sent an e-mail through his website anyway, and his secretary e-mailed a phone number back right away. We set up a meeting during his next visit to D.C. It all happened so fast. Can you believe it?"

Tara shook her head. "*I* can't. Gaithers is big."

"Okay," Sameera said. "*Who* is Jerry Gaithers? And why is he commenting on Sparrowblog?"

"Only one of the top agents in Hollywood," Miranda said. "His agency has represented nine Oscar-winning actresses. And he wants to meet with me here, in the White House."

"He does?" Maybe her cousin's dream of becoming a Hollywood hottie was about to come true. Too bad it was her aunt and uncle's biggest nightmare.

"Yes, and I hope it's okay that I invited him to come. Aunt Liz, his secretary told me that you'll have to be there, too, because I'm not eighteen yet."

Tara was tapping her stylus on the screen again. "What date are we talking about here?"

When Miranda told her, Tara shook her head. "You can't make it, Liz. You're supposed to be in Texas to speak at a teachers' convention."

"Can you switch the date, Miranda?" Mom asked.

Miranda's smile had faded. "I can't. His secretary said he was coming to town just for that one afternoon. I *have* to meet with him, Aunt Liz."

Sameera shot her mom a look, and Mom rose to the occasion. "Cancel that speech, Tara," she said grandly. "Jerry Gaithers—and my niece—trump the teachers. Book the fireside room; we'll even serve the gentleman some tea."

"Thank you, thank you, thank you," Miranda said, kissing her on the cheek. "You're the best aunt in the world."

"I'd better get back to being First Lady, girls, so that these good people can get home at a decent hour."

The cousins got the hint. "How did he find out that you want to act, Ran?" Sparrow asked, as they made their way up the staircase to the Residence.

"Don't you read your comments, Sparrow? Your friend Sangi posted a question for me a couple of days ago, asking what I was up to at the White House, how I was doing, what my dreams were, and stuff like that. I can't wait to meet that girl on Friday night; she's awesome."

"What? I don't remember seeing that at all." One of the things Sameera wanted to ask an expert blogger was how to process so many responses at once, both positive and negative. She was battling a tendency to skim over approval from the friendly visitors and focus on challenges from more controversial posters like Sparrowhawk.

"This was in a nested thread with Sangi and me going back and forth," explained Miranda. "You'd have to click two or three times to get to that level."

"Oh, no wonder. I hardly have time to read the comments, let alone responses to responses."

"Anyway, I answered Sangi by saying my dream was to become an actor. Gaithers's people must have read that."

"Wow. They're certainly scrutinizing Sparrowblog closely."

"This could be my big break, Sparrow. Do you know how much actors get *paid*?"

"Mom and Tara are still trying to find you a job here, Ran."

"Good. I need some money *now*. I'm glad Tara's on it; she's so organized and efficient, she's bound to find something."

"In the meantime, it looks like we might have found something for *her*," Sameera said. "Or someone." She explained her matchmakers-Tara-Colby plan to her cousin.

"Young Cougar . . . and Tara?" Miranda asked. "He really thinks she's hot?"

"Yep. Told me so himself. His name's JB, actually. Now we just have to figure out a way to get him to sit down and join us at dinner tonight."

"Well, good luck with that one. Sparrow, what if Gaithers asks me to audition something for him? Maybe I should start reviewing my lines from *Our Town* so I can show him what I can do."

When Maryfield's community theater staged a production of Thornton Wilder's play *Our Town*, Miranda was cast in the lead role. The county paper gave her a rave review; Maryfield was still buzzing about her outstanding performance.

"You go ahead and rehearse. I have to make a reservation for tonight. For four, because if we have an empty seat, JB will be more likely to sit down."

chapter 15

When the restaurant manager informed her over the phone that they were completely booked, Sameera decided to pull rank. If any woman needed help in the romance department, it was Tara Colby.

"Oh, of course, Miss Righton," the woman at the bistro gushed as soon as Sameera revealed her identity. "We'll have a table for four reserved for you at eight o'clock. Thank you for choosing our restaurant."

Miranda always took twice as long as her cousin to get ready, so while she waited Sameera scrolled through the long archive of comments on her blog. She tried her best to track layered side threads that spun off from her original posts, but some of them stretched on and on. Sparrowbloggers were apparently just as interested in what others had to say as they were in the First Daughter's thoughts. The conversation took odd turns, headed into uncharted territory, and lured casual surfers into heated discussions. *Good*, Sameera thought. She wanted Sparrowblog to be elastic, flexible, a work in progress created by many different hands. *And it's still a close race between fun people and serious people. Guess I'll have to keep providing both types of posts . . . oh, here's that comment from Jerry Gaithers. Or his secretary.*

She read the note, which seemed legit, and opened a new browser window to search for his name. Sure enough, he was a top-notch, hotshot agent in Hollywood, forty something, bald with a comb-over, just divorced from a third wife, who was in the process of suing him for everything. *Hmm, sounds like a charmer,* Sameera thought.

Miranda was finally ready, and the girls headed down to meet Tara. Inside the bustling bistro, Sameera followed Tara, Miranda, and the maître d', answering greetings from strangers who called out things like "Hey, Sparrow!" and "How's life in the House?" *At least they're all friendly,* she thought. *No hecklers in this crowd.*

Tara was still wearing the navy blue suit with white trim, her hair hadn't budged a centimeter since the afternoon, and her lipstick looked like it had been tattooed in place. "Why four place settings?" she asked as they sat down. "Are we expecting someone?"

Sameera elbowed her cousin; she hadn't thought through an answer to this obvious question.

"Oh, you know *everybody* in this town, Tara," Miranda said brightly. "We'll leave a chair so that your acquaintances can sit and chat for a while."

Tara looked suspicious but didn't say anything. The girls opened their menus and decided what to order. "I'll have a cappuccino," Tara said, sighing as she put her menu aside.

"That's it?" the waiter asked.

"Tara, you have to eat something," Sameera said. "Here—I'll order for you."

"Okay, but nothing too heavy," Tara said. "I don't have time to work out these days so it goes right to the hips."

Despite the empty chair at their table, the girls' match-making didn't progress during dinner. JB remained on task, standing vigilantly at the door with the other agents. He didn't look Tara's way once, and Tara certainly paid no attention to him. She was too busy gobbling down the Caesar salad with grilled salmon that Sameera ordered for her. Occasionally, she looked up from her plate and gazed into the distance, murmuring with pleasure as she chewed a bite of fish or a piece of romaine lettuce drenched in dressing.

When the waiter came to clear their table, Tara grabbed the unfinished basket of bread and butter from his hand. "I'm not done with that," she said.

Leaving their dinner companion blissfully buttering an-other roll, Sameera and Miranda excused themselves and headed past the agents on their way to the ladies' room. In a whispered aside, with Miranda blocking her from Tara's view, Sameera asked JB to join them at the table for dessert. He shook his head no without saying anything, while the other agent smirked knowingly.

"We'll have to bring up the subject with Tara," Sameera told her cousin as they washed their hands at the sink. "You get things started, and I'll follow through by asking if she'd go out with him."

"Right," Miranda said. "I'm all over it."

Tara was leaning back in her chair when they returned

to the table, a look of contentment on her face. The bread basket was empty; no trace of lipstick remained on her now buttery lips. *She certainly looks more relaxed,* Sameera thought. *Maybe the key to helping Tara enjoy life is to stuff her with calories. That's it—she's underfed AND underloved.*

"The photos of you in church on Sunday and walking Jingle on the South Lawn are great," Tara said, smiling. "It was a good idea to pose with the lab, Sparrow. Maybe you should join our brainstorming sessions—you've got quite a feel for what the public likes, don't you?"

"I didn't really plan to pose with Jingle," Sparrow admitted. "He chased a squirrel over to the gate, and I chased him."

The waiter brought over the Death by Chocolate dessert that Tara must have ordered while the girls were in the bathroom.

"I've been thinking," Miranda said, trying to sound natural. "Some of those Secret Service dudes are *cute*. I've got some stills on my camera that I could use to turn into a calendar—HOT MEN OF THE SECRET SERVICE."

"You're so right, Ran," Sameera added quickly. "That one over there, JB, is definitely a hunk. Not to mention the nicest guy in town. He was so sweet on our walk the other day, and I hear he's single, too."

"Girls, come on. You can't make a calendar like that, and you can't go after an agent," Tara said. "You're underage, and you'll get him in trouble."

"Oh, definitely, he's way too old for *us*, Ms. Colby," Miranda said. "But for the right single woman of say, thirty-something . . . he's definitely a catch."

"*You're* not dating anyone, are you, Tara?" Sameera asked, after what she hoped was a long enough pause.

Tara speared the last bite of the Death by Chocolate with her fork like a fisherman who hadn't caught anything all day. "No. I always seem to go for the wrong type," she murmured, her eyes closed as she chewed and swallowed. "I've given up. I'm going to dedicate myself to making your mother the most successful, popular First Lady in history."

"You can't work all the time," Miranda said. "It's not good for the soul."

"Not good at all," Sameera piggybacked, deciding to take the plunge. "How about going out with JB on your day off, Tara?"

Tara's eyes flew open. "What? Me? Oh no, I couldn't. *That* guy? And me? It wouldn't work. He's . . . And I'm . . ."

"He thinks you're beautiful," Sameera said.

Tara's eyes darted over to the door where JB was standing. Just then, the agent folded his arms across his chest and sizeable biceps bulged under the sleeves of his dark gray suit. *Good timing, JB,* Sameera thought.

"He said that?" Tara asked. "That . . . I'm *beautiful*?"

Pink cheeks, Sameera thought. *Good sign.* "Yep. That's what he told me earlier this afternoon."

"But . . . but . . ." Tara lowered her voice and her eyes darted around the room before she finished her sentence. "He's black . . . and I'm . . . not. I've never dated anybody who wasn't, well, white."

Sameera was shocked. She hadn't stopped to think about the fact that JB was African American and Tara was white. She was even more surprised to see her cousin nodding in understanding. But, of course, Miranda hadn't grown up in diplomatic communities where people from different cultures and races mingled without much fuss. Even Sameera's Turkish teammate and his Armenian girlfriend had eventually won their families' blessings.

"I know. That's what I thought when Sparrow first brought up the possibility, Tara. But—" Miranda was saying.

"What's the big deal?" Sameera interrupted, taken aback by her own intensity. "Why are people *still* stressing out about stuff like that?"

"Calm down, Sparrow," her cousin said. "I was just about to say that race definitely doesn't matter as much as it used to. JB's smart and strong and brave. If he were fifteen years younger, I'd date him in a heartbeat."

Tara was ogling JB again. He smiled at something the other Cougar said; they could see the dimples from all the way across the room. Sameera capitalized on the perfect moment: "How about it, Tara? I could give him your number if you wanted."

"Well . . ." Tara said, tearing her eyes away from the agent. "I suppose I could try one date. It wouldn't hurt. My ancestors would probably have a fit, but they can't do anything about it now, can they?"

"No, they can't," Sameera said firmly. "Ancestors have no power *at all*."

chapter 16

Sameera handed Tara's private cell phone number to JB the next day. "She wants you to call," she announced triumphantly.

The agent seemed taken aback, just as Tara had been. "*She* wants to go out with *me*?" he asked.

Oh no, Sameera thought. *It's the race thing again.* But she was wrong.

"Does she know about the kids?" he asked.

Sameera gulped. "Uh—no. How many kids do you have, JB?"

"Twins. They're in kindergarten. And I've got full custody."

"You do? What about their mother?"

He sighed. "Now that's a long, sad story. Too long for right now."

"Well, you don't have to bring the twins along on a date, do you? Get a babysitter, take Tara out for dinner, and talk. I'm sure she won't care that you have kids."

But JB looked skeptical, and Sameera didn't blame him. She couldn't imagine Tara Colby interacting with anybody under the age of twelve, let alone greeting a couple of kids after school with a batch of homemade chocolate chip cookies. *But then again, she'd whip the PTA into shape in no time,* Sameera thought. *Those other parents wouldn't know what hit them.*

"Tara's biological clock is ticking," she said encouragingly. "She might love the idea of kids. Besides, you'll never know unless you talk about it. Ask her out this weekend."

Sameera herself was waiting eagerly for the weekend. How could seven days crawl by so slowly? Bobby was flying out of Dulles airport on Friday afternoon. How soon was he going to be able to call her?

All that week, when the girls weren't studying or brainstorming ideas and ordering furniture for the rooms they were redecorating, Miranda was on Sameera's laptop, editing movie footage and adding music and other sound effects. Sameera tried peering over her cousin's shoulder a couple of times, but Miranda obviously didn't want an audience—at least, not yet.

"You can have your laptop back in an hour," she said, sounding annoyed. "I want to show you this when I'm done—not while it's in process. You're too much of a movie buff to see an unfinished product."

"Okay, okay! Wow, I'd heard that creative types get irritable when they're working, but this is ridiculous."

Miranda was also getting ready for her big appointment with Jerry Gaithers, Hollywood agent. "I just want to get a bit part in a movie or even a commercial," she said. "At least to start with. I wonder if Mom and Dad will let me move to California by myself."

"I'll go with you," Sameera offered. "We can get an apartment together. Me, you, and a couple of Cougars. Oh, and Jingle, of course." She reached down to ruffle his fur as he looked up at her adoringly.

"Sparrow! That would be wonderful. I'm so glad things are getting started *right now* while I'm still seventeen. Making it in Hollywood is all about *timing*. And connections, of course. And finally I've got both."

"Mom and Tara are still trying to figure out a way for you to earn some money inside the White House, too."

"That's fine, but I won't need a part-time job if Gaithers gets me a gig right away. *I'll* pay for Mrs. Mathews's salary next year; your parents have done more than enough already."

It was "Gaithers" this and "Gaithers" that. Sameera was getting a little nervous about Miranda's expectations. She hated to watch celebrity wannabes crying buckets when they were cut from shows like *American Rock Star*, but this was Miranda's dream, so she didn't say anything to dampen her cousin's anticipation.

Both girls were looking forward to hosting the SARSA

meeting on Friday night. Mariam had accepted the invitation with pleasure, somehow managing to talk her father into letting her come. Sameera couldn't wait to introduce Mariam to Miranda, and Sangi, George, and Nadia to Mariam and to her cousin, but she was hoping that none of them would ask questions about Bobby. She wasn't expecting to hear anything from him until late Friday night or Saturday, and she didn't want to explain why.

chapter 17

When Mom, Miranda, Tara, and Sameera headed out to visit St. Matthew's school on Thursday, JB was one of the agents assigned to accompany them. Sameera and Miranda sandwiched him while they were waiting for Mom and Tara in the East Colonnade.

"Did you ask her out yet?" Miranda asked.

"Not yet."

"JB! Ask her today! Or else we'll say something ourselves."

"Okay, okay, I'll try. I've been out of circulation for so long, I'm sort of nervous."

"I'll bet she does the hair thing," said Miranda.

"What hair thing?" asked the Secret Service agent.

"You know, when a girl likes a guy, she'll fiddle with her

hair while he's talking to her," Miranda explained. "It's a dead giveaway."

"Classic nonverbal," Sameera added.

JB laughed. "Sixteen-year-old girls are so sophisticated these days. Poor teenage guys don't have a hope."

"I'm seventeen, JB," Miranda reminded him.

"Oh, that explains everything."

Tara and Mom came out of the First Lady's office, and the cousins kept a sharp eye on Tara's reaction when she saw JB standing with them.

"Is the school ready for our visit?" Mom asked the agent.

"Yes, ma'am," JB answered. "Our team's already been there, and a couple of agents are waiting on-site. As it's an all-girl facility, I'll wait in the car, but two female agents will be present the whole time."

Tara looked up at him. "Oh. You're not coming inside with us?"

Sameera and Miranda both held their breath as one manicured fingertip reached for a strand of hair and started twisting it around a knuckle. "Yesss!" Miranda hissed into her cousin's ear. "He's good to go."

JB, too, seemed mesmerized by Tara's twirling finger, because he wasn't answering her question. Sameera nudged him gently with her elbow, and he cleared his throat. "Uhhh . . . What? Oh no, Ms. Colby, I don't want to invade female territory, now do I?"

"I'm sure the girls wouldn't mind," Tara said, almost purring. "And call me Tara, please."

Mom watched the whole interchange with growing interest. She had a knowing look as they settled into the back of the armored limo. "Nice work, girls," she whispered to Sameera and Miranda. "Definitely a step up from her last boyfriend."

"I hope you like my alma mater, Sparrow," Tara said, sliding in beside Sameera and closing the door. "It's the perfect school for a First Daughter."

"It's no place for the First Niece, that's for sure," said Miranda. "No guys? How did you stand that?"

Tara smiled. "Oh, we found our way around it, of course. There's a boys' academy around the corner, and I'll bet the same meeting places are fully operational—Jake's Grill and the Totem Teahouse."

The school was obviously in a state of excitement over the First Family's visit. Bouquets of flowers were everywhere, wood floors and desks gleamed with fresh polish, chandeliers sparkled as though they had no idea that cobwebs existed elsewhere on the planet. Sameera felt like she'd entered a movie about a girls' school in the 1950s—students in identical crisp white blouses and knee-length plaid skirts, teachers garbed in long, black robes, classrooms filled with rows of wooden desks facing clean black chalkboards, a pristine chapel that glowed with antique stained-glass windows. Everyone they met said exactly the right things, sounding eerily like they were reciting lines from a script.

"*The Stepford School,*" Miranda whispered in her cousin's

ear, referring to a remake of the old horror film about robotic human substitutes. "The headmistress even looks like Nicole Kidman." She'd brought her video camera, of course, and had secured permission to film the tour.

An impeccably courteous senator's daughter served as their guide. "Our school has a two-hundred-year history," she said as a bell rang and students moved to their next destination in orderly, single-file lines. "We receive a first-rate classical education, just as rigorous as in British schools."

First-rate? Rigorous? Sameera thought, fighting an irrational desire to bhangra wildly down the hall. *What girl our age actually talks like that?*

They passed a window that overlooked the school's tidy, walled-in front garden, and she glimpsed Tara and JB standing beside a stone fountain. She nudged her cousin and pointed. "Looks like he might be making his move," she whispered.

The PE teacher greeted them in the gym. "We heard you used to cox, Miss Righton," she said. "We'd love to have you join the team. Our autumn regatta is a longstanding tradition."

Sameera fingered the state-of-the-art cox box that the woman handed her; it would be great to be part of a team again. Why, then, wasn't she getting excited about the school?

They moved to the English department. "I see your cousin likes filmmaking," said a teacher, smiling into Miranda's camera. "We offer a class on editing and screenwriting, and a couple of students have won prizes at national youth film festivals with their final projects. We also have an award-winning newspaper, which I understand is one of your passions, Sparrow."

Sameera smiled and nodded, trying to cover her lack of enthusiasm. She'd been craving the excitement of being on a newspaper staff again. What was wrong with her now?

Their perpetually polite guide led them into the cafeteria, still reciting her memorized speech. The airy room, lit by sunshine pouring in through the floor-to-ceiling windows, was full of the savory aroma of oregano, melted cheese, sausage, and sautéed onions. While Miranda filmed one of the chefs chopping fresh fruit, Sameera drank in the lovely buzz of conversation as groups of girls laughed, argued, gossiped, and even sang in various corners.

Now this was more like it. Maybe this place had possibilities after all.

"Sparrow!" A student ran over with arms outstretched, a big smile of welcome on her face.

"Great to see you," Sameera said, trying to conceal that she had no idea who in the world she was hugging.

"Remember me? Brianna Farnsworth? From the father-daughter dance during the campaign? My friend and I met you in the ladies' room."

The light dawned. "You guys were the best that night. I ended up having a ton of fun."

They chatted until the bell rang. "I hope you decide to

come here in the fall," Brianna said. "But I'm sure we'll run into each other before then. All the political kids our age go to the same events and parties—you end up seeing each other over and over again."

Miranda grinned. "Sounds like a small town."

"Feels like it sometimes," Brianna said ruefully. "Especially when there's something juicy to gossip about."

After the rest of the tour, the tall, elegant, Nicole-Kidmanish headmistress served Sameera, Miranda, and Elizabeth Campbell Righton coffee in her office. " 'Timeless and traditional,' that's our motto," she said. "We'll do what it takes to keep your daughter safe, Mrs. Righton. Many senators and members of Congress entrust their girls to our care."

I've already got plenty of "timeless and traditional," thank you very much, Sameera thought. *I definitely don't need it 24/7.*

She could tell by the expression on her mother's face that a big question was coming, and she was right. "Do you teach many low-income students at St. Matthew's?" Mom asked.

"We have a few scholarship students, and we're always trying to increase our endowment for those purposes."

They stood up to leave, and Mom told the headmistress that they'd be in touch.

"So, what did you think?" Tara asked, meeting them outside in the garden. Sameera noticed that she was smiling like she'd just won an award for being the ultimate First Lady's first lady.

"This school is amazing!" said Mom overenthusiastically.

"The girls seemed really friendly!" said Sameera brightly.

"Seems like they've been doing the same thing the same way for years and years," Miranda said. Then she must have caught sight of Tara's smile dimming, because she quickly added, "Nothing wrong with tradition, though, as Gran likes to remind us. Right, Sparrow?"

I'm all for tradition, Sameera thought. *As long as it doesn't get in the way of changing things that need to be changed.* "I'm not sure it's the place for me," she said out loud. "But we don't have to decide right now. Let me check out a couple of other schools first, okay?"

"That's fine, Sparrow," Tara said, her grin returning to full wattage as though she couldn't stop it. "Hey, guess what I'm doing Saturday night?"

"Going out with JB!" Sameera and Miranda said it in unison, exchanging fist punches with each other, Mom, and even Tara herself.

chapter 18

Sameera, Miranda, and Jingle ventured into the chilly night air of the Portico. They were meeting the limo that the First Lady's office had sent to pick up Mariam. To Sameera's astonishment, Mariam's father emerged from the car instead of Mariam. He took one look at Jingle, who was emitting his usual effusive *bark-bark-bark* of welcome, and muttered something over his shoulder before hurriedly closing the door behind him.

"Uncle Muhammad!" Sameera exclaimed. "I didn't know you were—I mean, I'm so happy to see you!"

"You gave us quite the surprise when we learned your true identity, my dear," he said, nervously keeping an eye on Jingle, who was now circling him, tail wagging wildly.

"I know, I'm sorry I didn't tell you who I was the day we met, but I didn't want to worry you. Besides, Dad wasn't the president back then."

"Nonetheless, we are glad to know the truth now. And we shall never forget your kindness to my mother." He backed up against the car as the dog came closer to sniff him.

"This is my cousin, Miranda," Sameera said, and her cousin smiled and nodded at their visitor.

Uncle Muhammad nodded, too, but he was still plastered against the side of the car, eyes fixed on Jingle's every movement.

Sameera peered around him at the tinted glass of the window. "Didn't Mariam come with you?"

"Yes, but she's a bit . . . frightened about the dog."

"Let me put Jingle away, then," said Miranda, corralling the dog and leading him up the stairs.

A burka-covered figure crawled out of the limo and Sameera enveloped it in a huge hug. The last time she'd seen Mariam, the other girl had been wearing only a head scarf. This time she was fully covered.

"I'm so glad you're here, Mariam," Sameera said.

"Me too," Mariam answered.

"How is your mother doing? And your grandmother?"

"Quite well, thank you. They send warm greetings to you and your parents."

Uncle Muhammad looked a lot more relaxed now that they were dog-free. He crossed his hands in the air back and forth with the palms facing down, like a conductor at the symphony. "No need to bother your father this time to meet with me; I know he is a very busy man. Next time we will take some tea together."

"Oh. Dad's not here, actually. I think he and Mom are at a dinner event somewhere."

I have no idea where my parents are, she thought. She did, however, know that Bobby Ghosh had already landed in Charleston, South Carolina, and was probably having dinner with his parents. She'd thought about it all day. When would she hear from him? On Saturday? Sunday? When he got back into town? He probably didn't want to miss too many classes, so she figured the latest he'd get back would be Tuesday.

"No worries, no worries," Uncle Muhammad was saying. "He is a good man, your father. I would have voted for him if I could have. I will wait while you have your meeting. Mariam tells me this is a good chance for her to be discussing with college students."

"Come in, please. It's cold out here. I'll take you through security."

Sangi, George, and Nadia arrived on foot, from the George Washington University campus, which was only blocks away. After they, too, were wanded, IDed, and cleared, Sameera introduced everybody, delighted that Sangi gave both Miranda and Mariam warm hugs as though they'd known each other for years.

They took a quick tour of the ground floor of the Residence, accompanied by a couple of agents. Miranda trailed behind with the camera plastered against her eyeball; she'd asked permission to film and everybody had given it, even Uncle Muhammad, who'd agreed somewhat reluctantly.

Sameera's guests seemed strangely quiet as they walked through the famous rooms on the ground floor—the Library; the Vermeil Room, with its heirloom collection of gold-plated silver; the China Room, where the plates and glassware used by past presidents were on display; the oval Diplomatic Reception Room with its panoramic wallpaper installed by Jacqueline Kennedy. Even Sangi was subdued, awed, almost tiptoeing as they headed up to the first floor and walked through the expansive East Room, the Green, Blue, and Red Rooms, and the State Dining Room. Then, Uncle Muhammad was safely ensconced back downstairs in the Map Room with Mature Cougar keeping him company, while the younger people continued to the private part of the Residence on the second and third floors.

Once the tour was over, they settled themselves in the cozy Lincoln Office, and any constraint or quiet instantly evaporated.

"This room is decorated so beautifully," said Sangi, wriggling deeper into one of the new leather recliners. "It's my favorite, I think."

The cousins exchanged triumphant glances. The leather furniture had arrived the day before and melded beautifully with the reupholstered antique sofa. It felt good to prove Designer Danny wrong.

"*I* adore that solarium," said Nadia. "I want one."

"When do I move in?" George asked. "The Lincoln Bedroom is much more *me* than my dorm room."

Mariam was stroking Jingle's fur and gazing into his amber-colored eyes. "I've always wanted a dog like this," she said. "But my parents are terrified of dogs; I think some of the strays in their village might have had rabies."

"Which part of Pakistan are you from?" Nadia asked.

"A village near Islamabad," Mariam answered.

She wasn't in the least bit shy now that her father wasn't in the room. Sameera had worried that a sixteen-year-old might clam up around a bunch of college students, but Mariam seemed just as relaxed as she had been in her own home.

"I'm from Karachi," Nadia told her.

"You are not," said George. "You're from Massachusetts. That's where you were born."

"So how do you answer that question, then?" Nadia asked. "I know you get asked it, too, George: 'So, where are *you* from?'"

"I tell them I'm from my mother's womb," George answered. "No, I say I'm from Maryland. It's true. That's where I feel most at home. But I guess when I visit Kerala, it feels like home, too."

"They don't want to know where your home is, George, they want to know your *ethnicity*," Sangi said. "I tell them I'm Punjabi American. *No* hyphen, thank you very much. I have two distinct identities and the only thing fusing them is my very own self."

"But you were born here," argued Sameera. "Why can't you just say you're from California? Ran, put that camera away and join the conversation."

Ran pressed the PAUSE button but didn't lower the camera. "This is great stuff, Sparrow. Does anybody else mind if I film while you chat?"

Sangi shrugged. "Go right ahead," she said. "It's because I don't want to lose the Punjabi part of me, Sparrow."

"I answer only that I'm an American," said Mariam. "That's what Baba told me to say. He thinks I'll get in trouble if I mention the word *Pakistani*."

There was a brief silence. "And have you?" Sameera asked gently. "Gotten in trouble, I mean?"

"Not really. My mother and grandmother bear the brunt of it because they don't speak English too well. You know, Sameera. You saw it happen at that grocery store. Baba and

I don't get hassled very often. People used to try and pull my head scarf off at school, since I'm the only girl who wears one, but now everybody's gotten used to it."

"I sort of get the head scarf thing, but why do you wear a burka?" Nadia asked. "Do your parents make you?"

Mariam's eyes crinkled, and Sameera knew she was smiling at a question that was probably a familiar one. *It's amazing how much the eyes reveal,* Sameera thought. "I wear this because it gives me freedom," Mariam said. "It puts me in charge, because I get to decide who sees me and who doesn't."

Sameera glanced from her guest's burka to her cousin's camera and felt a rush of affection for both of them. *Dad was right,* she thought. "Let's eat," she said, leading the way into the private dining room, where two fresh-baked extra-cheesy pizzas had been sent up from the White House kitchen.

"Pass the chili pepper flakes, will you, George?" Sangi asked, once they were seated around the round dining table.

"And here's the hot sauce," Sameera said. She'd asked Jean-Claude to bring it up, knowing that most of her guests preferred their food on the spicy side. "So, Mariam, do you have any questions for SARSA?"

"Is it hard to get into George Washington University?" Mariam asked immediately. "I'd love to go to college, but my parents don't want me to leave home. So the schools around here are my only possibility."

"G-Dub's hard to get into—you need good grades and you gotta do well on the SATs," Nadia said.

"I've got those, but is it expensive?" Mariam asked.

"Yes, but there are plenty of scholarships," Sangi answered. "Are you involved in any extracurriculars? Those definitely help."

"That's the problem," Mariam said. "We don't have very many activities at my high school. Just football and track. And I'm not a good runner."

George lifted his eyebrows. "What about band? Newspaper? Or yearbook?"

"No. We don't have those."

"Art?" he persisted. "Clubs? Anything?"

"No clubs. We have to leave when the last bell rings. They lock down the building and the grounds by three o'clock every day."

Sounds like Sparrowhawk's school, Sameera thought.

"Feel free to use us as an extracurricular, Mariam," George offered. "Put SARSA down on those college apps."

"What *is* SARSA, anyway?" Mariam asked, as the cousins passed around scotchies for dessert.

"We're the South Asian Republican Students' Association," Nadia explained.

"But what do you do?"

"We arrange for guest speakers to come to GW and set up debates on campus and other events. We do fundraisers for certain causes. And we try to shatter stereotypes on campus by showing that Republicans can actually care about fighting injustice and helping the poor."

"Join us any time you want," Sangi added, smiling warmly.

"We usually meet at the Revolutionary Café right near campus. It shouldn't be too far from where you live."

"But . . . I'm not a Republican," Mariam said. "In fact, I'm not even a citizen yet. And I'm still in high school."

"Who cares? You're almost in college. You can come even if you decide to vote Democrat once you do get your citizenship."

"And if your father wants to join you, he can certainly have a cup of tea at the café," Nadia added quickly.

"Okay, I'll ask him." Mariam's eyes were sparkling, and Sameera knew that the SARSA circle was opening to pull her inside, just as it had done for her a few months earlier.

An idea came racing into her brain like Jingle tearing after a squirrel. "I should check out your school, Mariam," she said out loud. "It might be just the place for me."

Miranda lowered her camera. "What?! You've never been to public school in your life."

"Well, that's all the more reason why I should experience it. Why not try something new? Especially since I'd already have a friend there?"

"It would be wonderful for me, Sameera, but like I told you, it's not such a great school," said Mariam.

"So what? It's good enough for you, isn't it? Why shouldn't it be good enough for me?"

"I think it sounds like a fantastic idea," Sangi said. "But I don't think any First Kid has ever gone to a public high school."

"Good. I like breaking new ground."

"Would your parents let you do it?" Nadia asked.

"I don't know," Sameera answered. "What do you think, Ran?"

Her cousin looked doubtful. "You could always try."

chapter 19

"Why don't you join SARSA, too, Miranda?" George asked. He looked eager for an answer, and Sameera wasn't surprised. Her cousin's charms were tough for most guys to resist.

Miranda shook her head. "I'm not South Asian, remember?"

"So what? Your cousin is, and that means you're part of a South Asian family," George said. "We head out to the bhangra club every now and then and white faces bob around there all the time."

"Okay. I'll go if Sparrow goes."

"When can you join us next, Sparrow?" Sangi asked.

Maybe Bobby will come back with good news, and we'll be there together, holding hands, like a real couple. "I'm going to try and come soon," Sameera promised. "But since I'll be in civilian clothes, the Cougars will have to come along, and so will a bunch of Rhinos, probably. So if you don't mind being in the news, I'll be there."

"Bobby's the only one who seems worried about that," Nadia said. "*We're* all okay with it. When is he getting back, by the way? I can't believe he went to South Carolina again so soon after the holidays."

Sameera didn't answer; she didn't know any details about Bobby's return to campus the following week, but she certainly didn't want to admit it to Nadia.

"Oh, that reminds me," George said. He was carefully avoiding Sameera's eyes, she noticed. "Bobby called this afternoon. He's not coming back to D.C. At least, not for a while."

"What?"

"What?"

"What?"

"Who's Bobby?"

The last voice was Mariam's. Sameera had somehow managed not to participate in the lava of "whats" erupting from Nadia, Sangi, and her cousin.

"He's a friend of ours," George explained. "A member of the chapter. His grandfather's taken a turn for the worse, and the whole Ghosh family's heading to India ASAP. Probably to pay their last respects."

"Isn't he . . . going to miss classes?" Sameera asked, keeping her voice in the normal range with a superhuman effort.

"Definitely," George answered. "They might be gone for

a long time, and he'll have to take incompletes, but he didn't seem to care. Oh, and he told me to tell you, Sparrow, that he'll try to send an e-mail as soon as he can. Which might take a while, since his grandfather's so sick."

"You haven't heard from him then, Sparrow?" Nadia asked.

"Not yet," Sameera admitted, casually taking a bite of pizza. She felt like her heart had plummeted to the soles of her feet. The pizza in her mouth tasted like chalk.

Miranda glanced quickly at her cousin. "Since we seem to be done with our official meeting, you guys want to go bowling?" she asked. "And watch a movie?"

"I'd love to," said George. "Lead the way."

"I did cleanup last time, Sparrow," said Miranda. "I get to take our guests down while *you* stack the cart."

Thank you, Ran, Sameera thought, as her cousin gave her a loving smile and led their guests out of the room.

Sameera tidied up in a daze, hardly knowing what she was doing. He was gone. To India. Without a word of good-bye. Without even trying to call or write. Which meant his grandfather must be seriously ill. And after getting such bad news, she didn't blame them one bit if a forbidden romance was the last thing the Ghosh family wanted to discuss.

Still, it was crushing. Sameera felt exhausted, like a marathon runner getting to mile twenty-six and finding out that there were many unknown miles ahead. She managed to hold it together during the rest of her friends' visit, even going down with her cousin to see them off.

"I'll keep you up to speed on the school situation," she promised. "See you next Friday, I hope!"

"How are you doing, Sparrow?" Ran asked gently as they walked back upstairs. "Sort of a shock, wasn't it?"

"You can say that again."

He'd told George that he'd try to e-mail once he got there. But how soon would a note come? And what if he didn't ever manage to convince his parents that their relationship shouldn't be *verboten*? She wanted to reach out across the miles and comfort him, but right now Sameera Righton needed some comforting, too.

Miranda got the message. "Let me tuck you into bed, Sparrow. Come on, go get in your jammies. Jingle's waiting for you on the bed already."

"Will you read to me?" Sameera asked as they headed into her room. "You know, like you used to when we were little."

"I'd love to. I know, I'll read you something from that poetry book. Westfield says that poetry has a way of healing the soul."

"Got some more Teasdale for me?" Sameera asked. She changed into her flannel jammies and got into bed.

"Sure do. Here's one called 'Barley Bending.'"

Now that she was cozily tucked in, her cousin's soothing voice and the words of the poem seemed to untangle some of Sameera's sadness.

Like barley bending
  In low fields by the sea,
Singing in hard wind
  Ceaselessly;
Like barley bending
  And rising again,
So would I, unbroken,
  Rise from pain;
So would I softly,
  Day long, night long,
Change my sorrow
  Into song.

chapter 20

The next morning, Sameera followed her ever-filming cousin down to the kitchen on the main floor, feeling a little too much like a lonely lamb to stay upstairs alone. A group of Pandas were meeting around the big butcher-block table. Their faces lit up when they saw the girls. "Just the person we wanted to see," Mr. Phillips announced.

"I am?" Sameera asked.

"Not you," he said. "Your cousin. The First Lady's hosting an afternoon tea for a group of diplomats and their spouses."

Miranda put down her camera. "Sparrow and I don't have to be there, do we?"

"No, but remember that extra batch of frosted oatmeal cookies you sent down here for us? Well, I served a couple when the Swedish ambassador was visiting, and apparently she's been raving nonstop about them. Now everybody's expecting them to be served at the tea. Ms. Colby told me to make sure that those scotchies were on the trays."

Another Panda cut in: "We've tried to duplicate your recipe, Miranda, but we can't make them taste quite like yours. Would you mind baking some more for the tea?"

"I think the secret is the mi—" Miranda started to say before Sameera cut her off.

"Don't you usually pay a caterer's fee for stuff you order from outside?" she asked.

The Pandas exchanged glances. "We do have money for that in the budget, but since your cousin's part of the family, we thought—"

"That's okay, I'll—" Miranda tried again, and again Sameera interrupted.

"Making scotchies takes time," she said. "And Ran's really busy with studying, not to mention her filmmaking and stuff. How much could you offer her to cater ten dozen scotchies?"

Mr. Phillips smiled. "A caterer's fee it is, then." He named an amount that seemed more than extravagant to the girls; they communicated their delight to each other with almost imperceptible eyebrow lifts.

Miranda was about to accept their offer when Sameera intervened again. "And she can use the supplies in the kitchen, as well as bake them here?"

"Of course. Will you do it, Miranda?"

"I'd be glad to."

Miranda skipped up the stairs two at a time. "Who would have thought that a bunch of scotchies would earn me so much money? I might even be able to buy some moviemaking software that works on the desktop computers around here. And then you can have your laptop to yourself, Miss Sameera."

"How about if I give you an advance loan and you buy it today?"

Miranda laughed. "It's been hard, huh?"

"Agony," Sameera admitted.

"Okay, I accept. I'll order it right now. And I'll use the desktop to do it."

"Great," Sameera said, handing over her credit card. "I'm going to figure out a way to milk this cookie-making biz a bit more. Which reminds me—keep our family's secret ingredient to yourself, Ran. Nobody needs to know that it's the Campbell cows that are making the difference."

"Isn't it ironic that those cows are turning out to be such a blessing—even from a distance?" Miranda asked. "Especially after all the abuse I've heaped on their poor fat heads."

While Ran browsed around to find the software she needed, Sameera didn't waste time. She got on her laptop and designed a sheet of simple business cards, importing a free graphic of a plate of steaming cookies as a logo. MERRY DUDE DAIRY FARM FRESH COOKIES, the card announced, followed by Miranda's name, e-mail address, and cell phone number. Running downstairs, she filched a couple of sheets of card stock from an East Wing office supply closet and printed the graphic off when she got back. Then she cut the cards out carefully with a pair of sharp scissors. They looked almost professional, at least to her eyes.

Her cousin returned with a stack of papers in hand. "I downloaded the manual, too," she said. "The software I got is supposed to be state of the art. I sure hope I can figure it out."

"You're already up the learning curve now, Ran. Here, check these out," Sameera said, handing her cousin the cards.

"Wow, Sparrow. These are beautiful."

"Let's go ask Mr. Phillips if you can hand them out with the cookies at the tea," Sameera said. "I'm sure they'll get you tons of orders."

"I don't know," Miranda said doubtfully. "Anyway, you ask him. I'd feel like I was being pushy."

The girls went down to the kitchen again, with Sameera carrying her cousin's new business cards. "Would you let us tuck one of these into each basket of cookies or place them somewhere on the trays?" she asked Mr. Phillips. "I'm sure Mom's guests would appreciate being able to order some for their own events."

The head pastry chef looked carefully at the cards. "You girls work fast. I suppose we can do that. But if you start doing this for a living, Miranda, you'll have to bake in the small kitchen upstairs on the third floor and buy your own ingredients. We can't have the taxpayers funding your enterprise."

"Of course," Miranda said quickly. "I doubt I'll get any orders, anyway."

"I wouldn't be surprised if you got more than you can bake," he said. "Those are some of the best cookies I've ever tasted. And I've done my fair share of sampling, believe me."

The next item on the cousinly agenda was finding the fastest desktop computer in the White House that wasn't being used by anybody else and hauling it into the Lincoln Sitting Room. Sameera installed the new software, while her cousin stapled together the pages of the manual and began flipping through it. "It's going to be good having a computer to myself," Miranda said.

You can say that again, Sameera thought, taking her beloved laptop over to the couch to check in on her blog—and see if there was anything in her in-box from India yet.

There was nothing from Bobby, so she went to Sparrowblog. As she skimmed through the comments, she realized there was only one type of response that she absolutely hated, and it wasn't the critical stuff from the likes of Sparrowhawk. What she couldn't stand were the disgusting notes from lecherous types. A few trickled her way, but ever since Miranda moved into the White House, weirdos were leaving a flood of propositions for her cousin. As Sameera frowned and deleted a comment from yet another loonie who was intent on harassing Miranda, she noticed a response that popped up from a user named "BanforthJD."

"Ran! Get in here!" she called.

Miranda hurried into the room. "Is it Bobby?"

"No. Not yet. It's something for *you*, actually, from Thomas Banforth, the son of the senator who ran against Dad. Westfield had dinner with him the other day, remember?"

"How could I not? He is the hunkiest of hunks, as I told Westfield."

"Well, Mr. Hunky is cyberleaping to your side, girlfriend. Check it out." Sameera read the comment out loud: "To those of you making disgusting comments about the Rightons' niece: back off. Why should she be targeted because of your sick issues? Remember, it's a crime to prey on minors on the Internet. We can find you. Miranda, if you're reading this, keep your chin up, and remember what Euripides said: 'Public opinion has most shallow eyes.' My mother will be contacting the White House to invite your aunt to dinner soon. She's never forgotten how Mrs. Righton defended her during the campaign. All the best to you and Sparrow, Thomas Banforth."

"That should stop them cold," Sameera said. "I think I'll post an excerpt from that note in my sidebar so that it's constantly in sight."

"The hottest law student in the country," Miranda said, fanning herself with ten fingers. "And he's standing up for *me*." Sighing, she went back to the desktop computer, where she'd shifted all of her movies.

With Bobby still on the brain, Sameera decided to launch into a romance-oriented post that she hoped would engage the fun seekers as well as the more serious types. And maybe even send a subliminal message Bobby's way if he checked in on Sparrowblog from the other side of the world.

Okay, intergalactics. Here's my question of the week: How do YOU decide if that certain someone is the guy or girl of your dreams? My cousin tells me we need to pick three treasures, and if we find someone who has those, shut up and put up with the rest of their character traits. Read this poem called "*Appraisal*" and then hit your browser's back button to return here.

Are you back? Did you like it?

Well, if Miranda and the poet Sara Teasdale are right, we're supposed to focus on the treasures in another person's character. So here's the Sparrowblog challenge—complete the following sentence by choosing three single-word adjectives: When I find the one

for me, s/he will be_____, _____, and_____.
You can describe your significant other if you're
already in a relationship.

What are your three treasures? I'll tell you mine next
time. Remember, keep them short, clean, and to
the point. Peace be with you. Sparrow.

After she published the post, she picked up the poetry anthology and read "Barley Bending" aloud to herself again: "So would I softly, day long, night long, change my sorrow into song." *But how long do I have to wait? Come on, Bobby. Write that e-mail already. Change my sorrow into song.*

chapter 21

The second time around, Teasdale's barley poem turned out to be prophetic. Sameera only had to wait exactly one "day long, night long" after rereading it. An e-mail winged its way from Kolkata, India, to Washington, D.C. on Sunday. She found it when she logged on after lunch, once again breaking her own no-screens-on-the-Sabbath rule in the quest for Bobby news.

Her heart danced a mini-bhangra when she saw the sender's name appearing in her in-box. But would the letter bring good news? Maybe his parents had finally given him permission to write. Or was his grandfather gone? She ran her hands quickly through Jingle's coat a couple of times before opening the e-mail, trying to steady her nerves.

Dear Sameera, I'm sure George told you about our emergency travel plans. Our family's ghar (home) is in a rural area about a two-hour drive from Kolkata. Dadu's holding on, and he recognized Baba, Ma, and me, but he's so fragile. He's insisting on staying at home with around-the-clock nursing care because he hates hospitals. Baba's already upset the local doctor by comparing his treatment with the state-of-the-art medical care available in America. MY father's no diplomat, that's for sure.

Here's my other big news: I managed to download your entire blog, without comments, of course, formatted it, printed it off, and took it with me on the plane.

(*You did?* Sameera thought. *He did?*)

Ma read your posts on the way to London, and then handed them to Baba without a word. He devoured them on the London-Kolkata leg. "So

now do you see why I want to be her friend?"
I asked.

"Yes, I do," Ma said. "She's quite smart.
And she's not really a Muslim, is she? Her
parents go to church."

"That won't matter to my father," Baba said.
"She has Muslim blood; that's enough for him."

"But if she doesn't practice Islam, maybe
he'll be more understanding," Ma argued.

My father shook his head like he always
does when he thinks living in America is
wrecking me.

"Look," I said. "Sparrow and I want to get to
know each other better. I'm planning to write
her while we're in India, but I wanted you to
know about it so I wouldn't have to lie."

They exchanged one of those parental looks—you
know how married couples communicate tons of
stuff without talking? My parents aren't too
affectionate with each other, at least not in
public, but they're totally fluent when it
comes to that eye-talk thing.

"E-mailing her is all right, Bobby," Ma said, after a bit.

"Keep in mind, though, that we're going to India for your grandfather's sake," Baba added. "He's your main priority right now."

So I've got the green light on writing you, and I don't have to feel like we're sneaking around. Baba did ask me to wait until Dadu gets a bit more stable before saying anything to him about you, so I'll let you know how that goes. I love him, Sameera.

Can't receive e-mail very often, though. I took the train into Kolkata this morning and am sending this from a cybercafé. I'm not sure if and when I'll be able to get back here to check it. Depends on how things go with Dadu. Please think of him in your prayers. I can't wait to see you when I get back; I miss you every minute of the day.

Love, Bobby

Sameera read it through five times. Suddenly, she realized her third nonnegotiable.

Tenderness.

Sara Teasdale had saved the best for last in her poem—
"a tenderness too deep to be gathered in a word." And
when a guy confessed his love for his grandfather, and then
a few sentences later told you he missed you every minute
of the day, he definitely had tenderness to spare.

Suddenly, Elizabeth Campbell Righton appeared out of
nowhere, outfitted in her Sunday fleecy sweats. "Hear anything from Bobby?" she asked, plopping down on the sofa.

Sameera was silent. How did mothers *know*? Did God
give them a special kind of radar when it came to the love
lives of their children?

"Come on, sweetheart," Mom said. "Don't make me use
my executive powers to get information out of you. Something is going on with that guy and you want to talk about
it. I can tell."

Sameera nodded slowly. It was true, even though she
might have to repeat the whole discussion with her father.
She handed her mom the laptop with the note still open on
the screen. Good thing Bobby hadn't gotten too personal.
Her mother started reading just as Ran came into the
room.

"E-mail from Bobby," Sameera said tersely, and her cousin
immediately leaned over Mom's shoulder to read the note.

Sameera's mother finished first. "Wait. Let me get this
straight. *Dadu* means grandfather, right? Bobby's in India
because his grandfather's sick? And his parents don't want
him to date you because they think you're *Muslim*?"

"Right."

"But you're not Muslim, Sparrow."

"I am by blood. And that's what counts for them."

Miranda was done reading now, too. "I think it's the grandfather who's got the problem with Sameera's heritage. His parents sound like they might be more open to the idea of Bobby and Sameera if he . . . weren't around."

Sameera took back the laptop. "Ran! You can't be wishing that he'd die! That's harsh."

"I didn't mean that. I meant he sounds like one of those patriarch types who rules the clan with an iron fist."

"Well . . ." Mom said. "I have to admit that I wasn't too thrilled about you falling in love with a Hindu guy."

"What?" Once again, Sameera couldn't believe what she was hearing.

"I know you're not sure what you believe right now, but what if your faith gets more important to you as you grow older? You might be sorry you married someone with a completely different religion."

"Mom! I'm only sixteen. I just want to date the guy— not marry him."

"Well, I'm being truthful. Parents care about stuff like this."

Ran grinned. "And besides, remember what Gran always says—"

The three of them repeated Sarah Campbell's mantra on relationships: "Date to relate, and honor your mate."

Just then, James Righton came wandering in, yawning and stretching. "Nothing like a Sunday afternoon nap to get you ready for a week of life-and-death decisions. What's going on, ladies?"

Silently, Sameera handed *him* the laptop. "Reminds me of myself when I was his age," he said, when he was done reading. "My parents were just as strict. I couldn't date anybody they thought was *inappropriate*."

"Really? Did you ever defy them, Dad?"

He shrugged. "Maybe passively, by not ever getting serious with anybody until they were gone. That's when I met your mom, and the rest is history." He tugged gently on Mom's ponytail as he settled beside her on the couch.

"I think his grandfather and his parents actually want to arrange Bobby's marriage the traditional way," Sameera said.

"Not a bad custom," Mom said. "I'm sure Gran would love to help find husbands for you girls."

"I suddenly feel called to the convent," said Miranda.

"Our marriage was arranged," Dad announced.

"Get to the punch line, Dad," Sameera said.

"It was *divinely* arranged."

"Ouch!" Sameera said, but it had nothing to do with her dad's bad joke. Her cousin had stepped on her foot. Hard. *"What?"*

"Good time to confess," Miranda hissed into her ear.

Sameera's parents sat up, looking wary.

"What? Oh. Right. Mom, Dad, I have to tell you something."

Silence. Then, "We're all ears, Sparrow," said Mom.

"Fire away, sweetheart," said Dad.

She told them about her excursion to the SARSA meeting in Foggy Bottom, watching their expressions change from anger to disappointment to understanding to . . . was that a glimpse of a smile when Miranda chimed in with how she hadn't been able to enjoy her lime-and-salt-scrub *at all*?

But the reigning emotion turned out to be a stern and righteous anger. "Never again, young lady!" Mom said. "Something terrible could have happened."

"Not to mention endangering the jobs and well-being of the agents assigned to protect you," Dad added.

"I know, I know," Sameera said. "I feel terrible. That's one of the reasons I'm trying to fix JB up with Tara—to atone for my mistake."

Mom reached for her hand and pulled Sameera across to the sofa so she was sitting in between them. "You are our most precious possession, darling."

"It was stupid, I know, but—"

Dad finally allowed himself to really smile. "But love makes you do crazy things. I remember, Sparrow. When *we* were falling in love, your mother and I walked the streets of Islamabad one entire night during an Embassy high security alert."

Sameera felt immensely better and was even enjoying being squashed into a parental sandwich on the uncomfortable sofa. "Tara went out with JB last night," she said. "I sure hope the sparks flew for them, too."

Later, the girls cornered JB to get the scoop.

"So, how'd it go?" Miranda asked.

His face stayed blank.

"Last night? With Tara? Come on, JB. We're in agony here."

"Good. Fine. We had a great time. She's . . . terrific."

"How'd she respond to the news about your kids?" Sameera asked.

"She didn't. I didn't tell her."

"JB!" Miranda said. "You've got to tell her the truth."

"I know," he said, sighing. "But she's so interesting, and fun, and smart. Too good for someone like me. I don't think I'm going to ask her out again."

"You are so good enough," said Sameera. "She's lucky to get a date with someone like you."

He didn't say anything, but she saw the side of his mouth curve up in a quick smile and the dimple in his cheek deepen. "Thanks, kid," he said.

chapter 22

Sameera opened the door into the Oval Office and peeked in, but the room was empty. Her father had to be in here somewhere—it was Wednesday, the day he usually scheduled back-to-back meetings inside the White House. She walked across the oval rug tailor-made to fit the unusually large room. Every president got to choose a new design, and Dad had asked for a sand-colored background and a border that looked like ocean waves to remind him of his California surfing days.

Where was that chilly draft coming from? Sameera walked over to close the window overlooking the small, private garden outside the Oval Office. She blinked and rubbed her eyes. No, she wasn't dreaming. The president and First Lady were sitting on a bench, holding hands, huddled together against the cold. Sameera could hear them talking.

"I'd love to make a friend or two here in town," Mom was saying. "I'm getting kind of lonely, James."

Sameera suddenly remembered Thomas Banforth's comment about his mother inviting them to dinner. The senator wasn't at all supportive of the Republican party's platform, but who cared? If Mom needed a friend, it was time to make it happen. Maybe Thomas needed a nudge.

"I hear the previous First Lady and the vice president's wife became quite close," Dad said. "Too bad my guy's a widower."

"Yeah. You should have thought of your wife's need for friends instead of the good of the country, James. What were you thinking?"

"I should have. We need to calendar in a regular date night, Liz, so we don't catch pneumonia out here trying to get some privacy. I miss spending time with *you*, darling, just the two of us—"

Sameera tiptoed away and headed upstairs. *At least the*

course of love is flowing smoothly for some people, she thought, checking her e-mail for another message from Bobby . . . just in case he'd managed to get to the city and into the cybercafé again. But there was nothing.

She consoled herself by reading through the interesting comments about nonnegotiables that people were discussing on her blog. It was becoming a girls versus guys debate, with guys insisting that girls had set their standards way too high and girls contending that too many guys were putting *hot* and *sexy* down as their choices.

Sameera steered the conversation by tallying up the responses, which clearly showed that just as many guys had high standards and that plenty of girls were focusing on external attributes, too.

Let's stay away from the gender divide and focus on character traits. Remember, you want this relationship to last until you're ninety years old. Think sexy's going to matter then?

Immediately, a response came from Ms. Graves, the Maryfield town librarian who had been one of the founding members of Sameera's intergalactic circle.

Don't be ageist, Sparrow, my love. You don't stop feeling sexy when you get old. I can assure you of that.

Sameera grinned as she typed an answer to that thread.

I stand corrected, Ms. Graves. You are definitely the sexiest librarian over seventy on the planet. All eligible bachelors should send interested inquiries to me via Sparrowblog.

Her cousin came in to show her some fabric samples for the Camp David redo, and they argued over the combination of colors and textures until they found something they both loved. They were getting better at conserving old stuff and mixing it up with the new, and the results, they thought, were fantastic. Not to mention economical.

"We're talented, Sparrow. They should give us our own show—*Designer Sameeranda's Décor for People on Budgets Who Aren't Dummies.*"

"But we're failing in our other mission," Sameera said. "JB *still* hasn't called Tara for a second date."

"Tara definitely likes him," Miranda said. "She walked past him ten times the other day, but he didn't move a muscle. She even flashed him some leg on purpose, bending down so the slit in her skirt did that check-out-my-silk-stockings thing."

"But JB acts like he's one of those bobbies with the big furry hats who stand in front of Buckingham Palace—he doesn't even blink when she's around. Obviously, Tara wants to go out with him again, but he's scared to tell her about the kids. Why are men such idiots?"

"Speaking of men, do you think Senator Banforth will really invite your Mom to dinner?" Miranda asked. "She's a

Democrat, right? Not to mention that your father kicked her butt in the election."

"Not quite. It was one of the closest races in history. Besides, I don't care if Ms. Banforth's a Democrat or a Communist. Mom needs friends in this town. I overheard her telling Dad that she was getting sort of lonely."

"My plan is that Senator Banforth will invite us to come, too," Miranda said. "And *he'll* be there, and our eyes will meet, and . . ."

"I think Mr. Thomas Banforth has the three Fs."

"He probably does. But can you imagine my mother's reaction when I bring home the son of a Democrat? She'll hit the roof."

"Good. You get your Democrat, Bobby can have his Muslim, and Tara can walk off into the sunset with her African-American father of two."

"I haven't even met my Democrat yet, Sparrow."

"I think the Banforth family could use a friendly reminder that my mother would love an invite."

They approached their tutor the next day. "You've got to use your connections, Westfield. Mom needs friends."

"And so do I, Westfield," added Miranda. "*Male* friends."

"Don't you think Tommy Banforth's a little old for you, Miranda? You're sixteen—"

"Seventeen. Why does everybody keep forgetting that?"

"—and he's in law school."

"You're as bad as Aunt Liz, Westfield. I'm not talking

about *marrying* him. At least not yet. Just drop a hint about having us over for dinner, will you?"

The tutor promised, and Miranda gave her a big hug of gratitude.

"Forget the hugs," Westfield said. "Save me a batch of those scotchies you're baking tonight."

At the end of the week, Sameera decided to stay and help Miranda fill the order for the tea instead of heading to the SARSA meeting. Her cousin smiled knowingly as she mixed up huge batches of dough.

"Hey, if the fifth member of SARSA were there, you wouldn't be here with *me* on a Friday night. You'd be out on the dance floor, doing that twisty-wrist, hands-up-in-the-air bobbing thing you guys do."

"Next time I bhangra, babe, you're coming with. Remember what George said? You're part of a South Asian family, Ran. Now focus on your work. After tomorrow, you're going to have so many orders you'll be on your way to a wealthy, cow-free old age."

"Yeah, right. You're a journalist, remember, not a novelist. These diplomatic dudes and dudettes get wined and dined all the time by gourmet chefs. They're going to eat my cookies along with Mr. Phillips's biscuits and scones, and nobody's going to say a word about them."

"Ah, but Mr. Phillips isn't using Merry Dude Dairy Farm milk in his frosting, now, is he?"

Despite Miranda's low expectations, her scotchies came out perfect as usual, and the diplomats were delighted.

Every single one of the Merry Dude Dairy Farm Fresh Cookies cards had disappeared by the end of the tea. And to Miranda's amazement, she got her first order from the Brazilian ambassador before she left—two dozen scotchies to send to her son in college.

The girls waited until the guests were gone before they celebrated. "Move over, Mrs. Fields!" Sameera yelled, as she and her cousin Viennese waltzed triumphantly around the empty East Room. "Make way for Miranda Campbell and her Merry Dude cookies!"

chapter 23

Sameera's interest in seeing Mariam's school grew stronger every day. It wasn't that she had extra time on her hands or that life in the White House was getting dull. There were gala black-tie evenings to attend with her cousin and parents, where she got to show off her red convention dress and some of the other wonderful ensembles the stylist had put together during the campaign. She and Miranda joined Mom for the opening night of *Les Miserables* at the Kennedy Center, and the whole family enjoyed the thirteen-year-old piano virtuoso's Chopin concert at the National Cathedral.

During the day, they had Westfield, of course, and both cousins were busy with Miranda's cookie-making business.

They were also having a great time with their Designer-Danny-free redecorating scheme. Even Tara practically gushed over the way they'd done their rooms, the Lincoln Sitting Room, and their plan for Dad's bedroom on Air Force One. The entire Campbell clan was coming to Camp David for Easter, so the girls were busy finishing that project now. And while Miranda tinkered with her movies, Sameera moderated comments on her blog, chatted online with her newspaper buddies and crew team from Brussels, and talked on the phone with Mariam or Sangi. And fantasized about Bobby's return, of course.

No, she had plenty do. She loved the perks of White House life—what girl wouldn't?—but her desire to see Mariam's school kept intensifying. During her visit to Tara's alma mater, she'd realized the main reason she wanted to go to school again wasn't because of coxing or journalism. She missed mingling with people her age. And she wanted *all* kinds of friends—not just those with megapowerful parents. She was bound to run into St. Matthew's girls at political parties and upscale fundraisers, and over four years she might become friends with some of them. But how would she get the chance to know someone like Mariam better unless she stepped outside the First Daughter safety zone?

Finally, she couldn't wait any longer. "My friend Mariam's school is only about four miles away," she told her parents casually one Sunday evening. "What do you think about me checking out that place?"

"Isn't that a public school, Sparrow?" Mom asked.

Dad was shaking his head firmly and presidentially. "No way, Sparrow. The public schools around here have cops doing security checks at the door. Not to mention the fact that their test scores are atrocious. You can't be serious."

Mom, too, looked dubious. "No other teenaged First Daughter has ever gone to a public high school, darling. Your father's right—the schools around here are rough."

"But, the whole school will be safer with me there, thanks to my detail."

"No, Sparrow," said Dad. "Absolutely not. It's too dangerous. You won't get a decent education, and—"

"What about the kids who live in D.C. and don't have any other choice, like Mariam? Heck, if the orphanage hadn't taken me in, I'd probably be illiterate, living somewhere in a Pakistani village trying to make ends meet."

Elizabeth Campbell Righton winced as though it hurt to picture her daughter in that situation. "You don't have to save the world just because you're the First Daughter, Sparrow. Why not have fun for the next few years? There's nothing wrong with that."

Sameera smiled at her mother. "I'm Elizabeth Campbell Righton's daughter, that's why not. And I'm planning to have fun, too, don't worry."

It was Dad's turn to pace the floor in front of the fire, and Jingle followed him back and forth diligently. "I don't get it, Sparrow," he said. "St. Matthew's sounds like a wonderful place. Great crew team. Outstanding faculty. Other students who wouldn't treat you like a celebrity. An award-winning newspaper. Why not go there?"

"I want to keep making different kinds of friends, Dad. Besides, I've done crew and newspaper already, but I've never been to a public school. The kids there will get over the fact that I'm famous once they get to know me."

"The Carters enrolled their daughter in a local elementary school," Dad said. "I remember seeing a picture of her walking there with a pack of reporters chasing her. I wouldn't want that to happen to you."

"You've seen the way I can handle the press," Sameera argued. "I'm sixteen, Dad. Almost seventeen. Not nine, like Amy Carter was."

"You haven't talked about academics, Sparrow."

"I'll be able to write about this experience, Dad. I could use it in my college essays. What admissions committee wouldn't respect that? And maybe Westfield can keep tutoring me after school."

Again, that parental exchange of glances. *This is exactly what Bobby was talking about,* Sameera thought, watching them closely and trying to read the signals.

"The only way we'd let you enroll in a school is if I get to see it first," said Mom finally. "As a mother—not as the First Lady so that they don't tidy things up just for my visit. I want to see the place *raw*, like any other parent."

Sameera didn't hesitate. "I know how we can swing that, Mom. Ever hear of a burka?"

"Of course I have, Sameera, but you're not thinking of trying that stunt again, are you?"

"Only if you try it with me. If we get you some brown-tinted contacts, both of us can go into Mariam's school incognito."

"What? That's impossible, Sparrow."

But James Righton was nodding. "Sounds like a good way to see the school without the school seeing you. It's innovative. I like it."

"But what about security, James?"

"This time we'll get the agents to work with us instead of trying to sneak off behind their backs," he answered. "Right, Sparrow?"

"Right. One of the Cougarettes has dark skin and brown eyes—we'll get a burka for her, too," Sameera said, brainstorming feverishly. "Mariam can tell her principal that she's got some visiting friends who want to see an American school. That would be true, wouldn't it?"

"But how would we get *out* of the White House and *into* the school without the press following us?" Mom asked, but Sameera could tell she, too, was starting to warm up to the plan.

"I don't know," Sameera said. "But I'll find out. And I know just who to ask."

"There is a secret passage," JB admitted reluctantly, when they called him up for a consult. "You can use that to get out of the building without the press discovering that you're leaving."

"Great," Mom said. "Let's check it out right now and see if it works. Lead the way."

"Right now?" JB asked.

"Now," Dad said firmly.

JB tried explaining to headquarters what they wanted to do, but Dad himself had to get on the phone before the top Secret Service honcho authorized the outing.

Followed by about six other agents, JB led them through a door in the hall between the bronze busts of Churchill and Eisenhower. They cut through a storage room and emerged into a hallway right by the White House florist.

At the end of the hallway, they took a sharp right. "Isn't this the way to the basement?" the president asked.

"It is," JB said, steering them through a steel door. When he opened it, all the nonagents gasped. There was a hidden tunnel that led under the East Wing away from the White House.

"Not too many people know about this exit," JB said sternly. "Let's keep it that way."

When they came out of the tunnel, they looked around blankly. "Where are we?" Mom asked.

"In the Treasury Building, next door to the White House," JB said. "It's closed now, since it's Sunday, but if you ever want to use this route for an unseen getaway, we can arrange to have a limo waiting around the back."

"Okay, Sparrow," Mom said. "I'll get those contacts."

"You can borrow my bronzing lotion, Aunt Liz," added Miranda.

"And I'll call Mariam right away," said Sameera.

chapter 24

The big public school visit had to wait until Mom got back from the teachers' conference in Texas. Tara had switched the day of the First Lady's keynote address so Mom could be with Ran when she met Gaithers. Meanwhile, Dad was leaving for London for a whole week.

Miranda invited Tara up to consult on an outfit for her big meeting with the Hollywood agent. "I don't want to look too young, Ms. Colby," she said. "Or like I'm trying to look too much older, either. It has to be just right—sophisticated and confident, but fresh and trendy at the same time."

Tara rifled through the clothes hanging in Miranda's closet and picked out a pair of caramel slacks, a matching blouse, and slim gold belt. Then she went across the hall to borrow Elizabeth Campbell Righton's brown suede blazer and a pair of high-heeled chocolate suede boots. Sameera watched critically—wouldn't her cousin look too plain in all that brown? But once Miranda was dressed, with her long blond hair combed straight over her shoulders, a small gold cross at her throat, and red, red lipstick, all three of them were satisfied.

"This is perfect, Ms. Colby," Miranda said, checking herself out in the mirror. "It's so . . . Hollywood."

"Without being totally starlet wannabe," added Sameera. "He's going to be impressed."

"How was your date with JB last Saturday, Ms. Colby?" Miranda asked. The girls were curious about her take, even though JB had told them he'd had a great time.

The usually poised older woman blushed. Actually blushed. "He's amazing," she said. "Now if you'll excuse me, girls, I've got work to do."

"She was starry-eyed," Sameera said, smirking.

"Sort of like you were the last time you saw Bobby."

"Yeah, but he has to tell her the truth about his kids, Ran."

Miranda's attention shifted back to her appointment. "Why don't you wait up here for me, Sparrow?" she asked hesitantly. "I'll—er—I'll let you know how it goes, okay?"

Sameera raised her eyebrows. "Why? I want to be right there with you. I can't wait to hear what Gaithers has to say."

"Sparrow, I don't . . . I mean . . . he wants to meet just with me, I think. And your mother."

"Please, Ran? I'll be as quiet as a ladybug, I promise. Hey, why didn't they name me that instead of Peanut? I wouldn't mind being called Ladybug; it's better, don't you think? Anyway, I won't say a word."

"Yeah, right. That would be a first."

Sameera felt a bit hurt. "When do I ever take over a conversation, Ran?"

"How about all the time? You've got lots of opinions, Sparrow. And lots of words. You're a journalist, remember? Don't get me wrong—I like it, usually, but . . . well, it's *my* day today."

"Mom has as many strong opinions as I do, and you want *her*."

"I know. But that's not my choice. Gaithers's secretary insisted that your mother had to be there. I would have liked to meet with him alone, actually."

"Forget the ladybug. I'll be as quiet as a Cougar, I promise. You won't even know I'm there."

Miranda sighed. "Okay, Sparrow. Come along, then."

Sameera found it excruciating to keep her promise to stay silent, as it turned out. First of all, Gaithers was late. Mom and Miranda paced by the hearth until someone came in to announce that their guest was getting his security clearance.

Miranda tried two different poses by the mantel. "Which one?" she asked Sameera anxiously.

"They're both fine. You're beautiful."

Minutes later, JB escorted in a short man wearing a gray suit and black turtleneck. Sameera took a quick look; this visitor had to be Gaithers, even though he looked ten years older than the photos she'd found online.

Their visitor strode away from the agent, who'd stopped just inside the door, and headed straight for Mom. "Mrs. Righton, I am so thrilled to meet you," he said, grabbing both of Mom's hands and ignoring Miranda and Sameera completely.

"We're glad to meet you, too, Mr. Gaithers," Mom said, taking the briefest of steps backward as the short man gazed up into her face.

"Let me cut to the chase," said Gaithers, still clutching Mom's hands and moving even closer. "My people have heard rumors that you might be trying to make the movie rating system your issue of choice during your husband's administration. I came to beg you to reconsider on behalf of the entire entertainment industry."

"You've heard that, have you?" Mom asked, easing her hands out of his and surreptitiously smoothing her palms against her skirt. "And you wanted to come here and talk about it? That's interesting. I thought that option was part of a private discussion that only my office staff knew about. And that you came here to meet my niece—not me."

"Let's keep things on the table, Mrs. Righton. I'm known as a straight talker, which is one of the reasons I've made it in this business. If the First Lady starts an anti-entertainment crusade, we stand to lose—"

"A lot of money," Mom finished. "Well, that's unfortunate, Mr. Gaithers, isn't it? Now, don't you want to meet my niece?"

Sameera was literally biting her tongue to keep herself from leaping into the conversation. She noticed that her mother didn't reveal the fact that she'd settled on her domestic issue just a couple of days before—to provide America's homeless children with shelter, education, and a hopeful future. Mom and Tara and the rest of her staff were working on the details of releasing the news to the media.

The First Lady's frosty tone of voice must have registered with the agent. His eyes scanned the room until they found Miranda, who had listened to the conversation without moving a muscle. "Of course I came to see your niece," he said. "Meredith, right?"

She's Miranda, *you idiot,* Sameera thought, fighting hard to keep the words from hurtling out of her mouth.

"It's Miranda," said her cousin.

Gaithers started walking around Miranda slowly, reminding Sameera of a tourist circling a statue. "Oh, she *is* lovely. I've been watching the news coverage, and she simply lights up a screen when the camera finds her, doesn't she?"

Why is he talking about her like she can't hear him? Sameera thought. *This guy's a loser, Ran. Can't you see that?*

"Thank you, Mr. Gaithers," Miranda said. "I've been acting in community theater since I was little. Would you like to hear me audition?"

He gave a short, condescending snort that might have been a laugh. "Definitely not. It's the visuals I care about, and you've certainly got those. Call my secretary to set up a photo shoot the next time you're in California. Here, take this."

He handed Miranda a card and turned back to the First Lady. "Mrs. Righton, I hope you reconsider which battles you plan to fight. I have a lot of friends in the industry who'd love to help the president get his job done. Not to mention see that young girls like your niece get a shot at their dream."

He doesn't need your help, Sameera thought. *And neither does Miranda.* "James grew up in California," Mom said curtly. "He's got plenty of support in Hollywood. Thank you for coming, Mr. Gaithers."

Miranda glanced at the tea table set for four, but Mom took their visitor firmly by the elbow and led him to JB. "Can you make sure Mr. Gaithers finds his way safely out of the White House, JB?" Mom asked.

"I'd love to, ma'am," the agent answered with conviction.

Once they were alone, Miranda let loose. "Aunt Liz! You were so . . . so unwelcoming!"

"I know, Miranda. I'm sorry. I couldn't take another minute with that man."

The two red spots burning on Miranda's cheeks reminded Sameera of stop signs. "Well, it's easy for *you* to blow him off! You'll never have to worry about money in your life—or ever go back to milking cows. Thanks for blowing *my* one shot at leaving!"

"Calm down, Miranda," Mom said, taking a sip of ice water. "He told you to call his secretary. James has plenty of friends in California; I'm sure we can find a place for you to stay if you'd like to pursue this."

Sameera shot Mom a surprised look, but still didn't say anything. She was going to keep her promise to stay quiet if it killed her.

"I know you don't want to be a dairy farmer for the rest of your life," Mom continued. "I get that. I'm hunting around for some meaningful work for you in the White House, but as I said, if you want to go after this opportunity, we can make it happen."

"I just might," Miranda said firmly, but the spots began to fade. "I'll let you know."

"I'm hungry," Sameera blurted out, sitting down and helping herself to a raspberry scone with clotted cream. It was exhausting to keep herself from using words; she'd never realized how much she relied on them.

"Me too," said Mom, sitting down and pouring the tea. "Come on, Miranda. I'm on your team, remember?"

Miranda sat down, her anger disappearing like the clotted cream on Sameera's plate. "Okay, Aunt Liz. He *was* kind of a jerk, wasn't he? I guess it wouldn't hurt to send some photos, though. Anyway, thanks for having him here."

Those Campbell women, Sameera thought, remembering her grandmother's volatile temper. *They get riled up quickly, but they cool down just as fast.*

chapter 25

When the First Lady and her entourage got back from their Texas visit later that week, Mom was flying high. Her No American Child Without a Home initiative (NACWAH) had been received with much support and delight by the teachers. Now she was planning to focus on her refugees overseas who'd been neglected for a while.

Meanwhile, the press was fawning over Sameera's father as he hobnobbed with the Prime Minister and royalty in London. *"Finally,* we have a president with the savoir faire to impress the America bashers in Europe," gushed a morning talk show host who seemed entranced with Dad's trim, handsome appearance in tails and top hat at Buckingham Palace.

The Residence's private phone rang that night, and Miranda picked it up. "It's for you, Aunt Liz," she said, her voice breathless and excited. "It's Senator Banforth."

"Victoria Banforth? For me? I wonder what she wants."

The girls could guess. They exchanged grins as they overheard the First Lady accepting the senator's invitation to Sunday supper.

"Since your father's gone, I thought it might be fun," Mom said, after the conversation was over.

"Definitely, Mom."

"Yeah, great idea, Aunt Liz."

The girls' voices were suspiciously casual, and Mom gave them one of her long squinty-eyed looks, but neither of them broke down and confessed.

Senator Banforth told Mom that she was planning to wear jeans, so the girls and the First Lady dressed casually. Sameera noticed her cousin taking extra care with her mascara and lipstick, and trying on about eight pairs of earrings.

"I'm meeting my future husband, Sparrow," Miranda said. "Take some footage with my camera, will you? I want to document this historic night for our kids."

When they walked into the senator's elegant colonial Virginia home, Sameera was overwhelmed with frustration on her cousin's behalf. Thomas Banforth had invited another guest to Sunday supper—Kaylie, a tall, slender brunette, who was a fellow student of his at Georgetown Law School.

"Why is *she* here?" Sameera hissed into Miranda's ear.

"No worries," Miranda whispered back calmly. "She can't thwart destiny."

Kaylie didn't seem impressed by the First Lady, First Daughter, or the First Niece. She commandeered the conversation easily, describing how she was putting herself through law school by modeling swimsuits for a catalog. The company she worked for was family friendly, she reassured them. "Just like your husband's administration, Mrs. Righton."

Tommy's mother, in return, didn't seem impressed *or* reassured by her son's date; Sameera watched her take stock of her guest's low-cut minidress and black fishnet stockings. *That outfit's going to be mighty distracting in the courtroom,* Sameera thought. *I'll bet nobody notices the murderer she's defending.*

But despite all the scenery Kaylie had to offer, and the fact that she probably had the brains to match, Miranda was right not to worry about the competition. Sameera noticed Kaylie's spiky-heeled foot caressing Tommy's ankle under the dinner table, but all through the meal he shifted his chair progressively away from his date's and closer to Miranda's. By the end of the evening, Tommy and Miranda were at the piano together, singing through his mother's hymnal. Meanwhile, Miss Swimsuit sat glowering on the couch as Senator Banforth tried convincing Mom to join a Bible study for women that took place on Capitol Hill.

Sameera, too, was sitting quietly in an armchair, fighting an intense bout of Bobby deprivation as she watched her cousin and the senator's son.

"It's a completely bipartisan group of women," Senator Banforth was saying. "We keep prayer requests confidential, and we support one another in other ways, too. You need friends you can trust to survive this job, Liz."

"I know," Mom said. "Whoever said it was lonely at the top must have been a First Lady. I'll come, definitely."

"Did Tommy go to public school, Senator Banforth?" Sameera asked suddenly.

"Call me Vicky, my dear. Yes, he did, but we live in McLean, remember? The D.C. schools are different. I think the Clintons might have considered it for Chelsea, but it would be tough to be the First Daughter *and* the only white person in the entire school."

Yeah, well, I'm not white, Sameera thought. *So I can go where no First Daughter's ever gone before.*

"Your son seems to have turned out okay," said Mom. "And he grew up in the limelight. You started this when he was about three, right? How'd you get through those tough teenage years?"

Sameera rolled her eyes. Like *she* was tough.

"The only thing I did right with Tommy when he was a teenager was letting him learn from his mistakes—and being there to bandage up any wounds."

"What mistakes, Mom?" her son called from the piano, where he and Miranda had stopped playing to eavesdrop on the conversation. He burst into a song at the top of his lungs, and Miranda joined in heartily: "Victory in Jesus, my Savior forever . . ."

Kaylie rolled her eyes and looked at her watch. "Look at the time, I've got to go," she said quickly. Sameera had almost forgotten she was there.

"Tommy!" Senator Banforth called. "Your guest is ready to leave."

The two-person choir came into the living room, with Tommy looking sheepish. "Sorry, Kaylie. Those hymns totally remind me of my childhood. They help me relax, and what with the pressure of papers and projects and stuff, I definitely need to do that. Want to come join us?"

"That isn't how I usually spend my free time," Kaylie said haughtily. "I'll drive myself home. It's a good thing we brought my car instead of yours. Thanks for dinner, Senator Banforth. It was lovely to meet you, Mrs. Righton." Her tone belied the words.

"I'll drive you back to your apartment later, Tommy," Senator Banforth said smoothly, getting Kaylie her coat and escorting her to the door. "Thanks for coming, my dear. God bless you in your studies."

Once again, Miranda and Sameera exchanged glances that would have included jubilant fist punching if they'd been alone. After Kaylie was gone, Tommy and Miranda headed straight back to the piano and resumed their hymn-sing as though his date's departure had been a minor blip in their perfect harmony.

"I'm a regular Sparrowblog reader, you know," Senator Banforth said as the three of them settled back down in the living room. "I even tried to come up with my own list of three treasures, but I had a hard time."

"I did, too," Mom confessed.

Sameera was astounded. "You guys both read that post?" First a random Austrian guy, now Senator Banforth, and even her own mom. Just how far did her intergalactic circle extend?

"Thomas got me hooked on Sparrowblog," Senator Banforth admitted. "Even during the campaign, I read it regularly. The comments are especially fascinating, aren't they?"

"I browse through Sparrowblog all the time, sweetheart," added Mom. "And so does your dad. I even comment sometimes, as *anonymous*. So what was on your list, Vicky?"

"I had a long one when I was younger, I'll tell you that much. But now I only have one thing on my list."

"What's that?" Sameera asked.

"A contrite spirit," the senator answered.

Mom was nodding knowingly. "I hear you," she said.

"Why is that so important?" Sameera asked.

"It's the ability to admit when you're wrong and a desire to change all bundled up together," Mom explained.

"You get mellow with time, Sparrow," Senator Banforth said. "We single gals over fifty aren't as picky as we used to be."

Mellow? Sameera thought. *Or desperate? Don't go chasing after any contrite convicted felons, Senator.*

"The amazing thing, my dear," the older woman was saying, "is when your short lists match."

"You mean if both of you pick the same qualities?" Sameera asked.

"You got it. If your top nonnegotiables mirror his, that's when you know he's a keeper. Even two out of three would be a good indication of compatibility."

I'll have to share that nugget of wisdom with my intergalactics, Sameera thought, wondering how high courage, honesty, and tenderness ranked on Bobby Ghosh's list.

chapter 26

Sameera was starting to feel at home almost everywhere in the White House. She began wandering down to the press corps room to chat with the journalists and bloggers who were there 24/7. To her relief, they seemed to consider these conversations off the record; it helped that she always brought along a carafe full of hot, fresh-brewed coffee and a plate of Miranda's scotchies. During one visit, she gathered her courage and approached one of the seasoned investigative reporters assigned to cover her father's presidency.

"Hello, darlin'," he said, flashing a dimple in his cheek. John Malone was renowned as a flirt, and having a midlife crisis to boot. She'd heard rumors that he was serially dating every young blogger on the White House beat. But he was also supposed to be one of the best reporters in the country.

"Listen, Mr. Malone, I was wondering something. Does

an idea ever get hold of you like it's . . . a Labrador and you're a bone?"

He grinned. "Great image, Sparrow. Yes, it does. It gnaws away at you and doesn't leave you alone. Why? Something got your interest?"

"Yeah. It's a . . . place I want to see for myself. And write about."

"You sound like a journalist to me. Did you ever hear of a reporter named Daniel Pearl?"

"Of course." Daniel Pearl was kidnapped and killed in Pakistan while on duty, and somehow the fact that he'd died in the land of her birth had always made it seem to Sameera that they had some kind of connection. If Pearl could pass the journalistic baton to her from the unseen realms, she'd take it with both hands.

"I knew him," Malone said. "And that's how Pakistan grabbed him. It held him by the jaws and wouldn't let go. We warned him about how dangerous it was to go there, but he went anyway. He got to know good people. He wrote his heart out. And he made a strange, new place feel like home."

That's what I want to do, Sameera thought. *Get to know good people. Write my heart out. Make a new place feel like home.*

As soon as her father got back from London, Sameera got things going. First, she asked Tara Colby to invite Uncle Muhammad and Mariam back to the White House. This time, Mariam's mother came along and so did her grandmother. Clad in burka and full head coverings, they both hugged and kissed Sameera, but everybody could tell they were overwhelmed with shyness at meeting the president and the First Lady.

Mom and Dad, who each knew a few phrases in Urdu, exerted their diplomatic skills to set their visitors at ease. Soon everybody in the room was chatting, with Mariam translating like she worked for the United Nations.

Mariam's mother had brought along a couple of burka for Mom and Sandra, the Cougarette who'd be accompanying them. Before leaving, Mariam's grandmother demonstrated how to move without tripping over the voluminous folds, while Mom and the agent watched dubiously.

"I'll have to practice," Mom said.

"Me too," said the Cougarette named Sandra. "Wearing that outfit looks tougher than some of the training I had to go through to become an agent."

"My brown-tinted contact lenses came," Mom said. "I'm thinking of wearing them every now and then just to throw people off."

"You must be turning more brown all over," Mariam's mother said, putting her hand next to the First Lady's to demonstrate the difference.

"I will be, don't worry. My niece is taking care of that."

By the end of the tea, plans for the big school visit day had been set. Uncle Muhammad would speak to the principal and set up the visit without letting him know the identity of the *observers*. The Cougars were going to make sure everybody followed appropriate security protocol, and had code named the event SVD.

"Sounds like a disease," Miranda muttered in her cousin's ear.

"*Phir Melenge,*" said Mariam's grandmother, meaning "we'll meet later" in Urdu, and Sameera felt a pang. That's how Bobby sometimes said good-bye, too.

She was longing for another e-mail to arrive from him. No news either meant his grandfather was still alive or that Bobby couldn't get to the city or the cybercafé. Sameera asked for prayer for the Ghosh family every Sunday at church, wishing she could somehow get an update.

It was so hard not to talk or write to him. She couldn't send a sympathy note, describe her public school adventure in the making, share how excited she was over her cousin's emerging cookie business, describe their innovative old and new decorating schemes, or just confess how much she missed him. *I'm starved for words,* Sameera realized. *Words from him to me. Words from me to him.*

chapter 27

When SVD finally arrived, Sameera couldn't help feeling nervous, despite the fact that she was experienced at heading out in public in disguise.

"I'm sorry you can't come with us, Ran," she told her cousin.

"I'd like to film the whole thing," Miranda admitted. "Those outfits hide a lot, but I doubt I could hide a camera under a head covering."

"I wish I didn't feel like I had to pee," Sameera said. "Remember during hide-and-seek how we always felt like going to the bathroom when it was time to hide? Well, that's exactly what's happening to me today."

Mom didn't seem worried at all. "I feel like we're in a Bond flick," she said, humming the theme song from the movies as she, Sameera, and Sandra stole through the secret tunnel and into the Treasury Building. A taxi was waiting around the corner with JB beside the driver, who was an undercover agent dressed like a cabbie.

"Remember, Mom," Sameera warned. "Don't *say anything*, or someone might recognize you. And don't wash your hands if you have to go to the bathroom. I'm not sure how waterproof Miranda's bronzer is."

"Don't worry. I won't go to the bathroom. I'm going to remain totally silent and let you answer any questions that come our way with that amazing Pakistani accent you do. Your tongue wraps around those retroflex *t*'s and that impossible *dhuh* sound—impossible for me, that is. *You* sound like the real thing."

I am the real thing. "I'm not going to say anything either," Sameera said. "Mariam's going to handle the questions. She'll translate them into Urdu, we're going to pretend to understand, and then she's going to make up some answer."

"I hope she's not going to have to lie on our behalf. I'd hate that."

"No way. Mariam's an expert in telling the truth without betraying secrets. Her parents are so strict, she's got it down to an art."

They were there. It was time. Sameera took a deep breath. This was no Bond movie; this was real. If they didn't pull it off, the First Lady and First Daughter could end up getting tarred and feathered in the media. Mom's eyes suddenly looked as anxious as Sameera felt, and they clasped each other's hands as they climbed the stairs to the main entrance of the school.

A female security officer scanned them from head to toe with a metal detector, and cleared them to enter the building. The principal was too busy to stop and talk, but he smiled when Mariam introduced them and said he hoped they would enjoy their visit. Sameera felt herself relax a bit. If he wasn't wary or suspicious, maybe nobody else would be, either.

People stared, of course, as three burka-clad women followed Mariam from class to class, and a few students asked questions. But when Mariam answered briefly that these were guests who wanted to observe the school, nobody pursued the subject.

Sameera started taking in the sights, sounds, and smells of Jacob Lawrence High School. The halls were narrow, the classrooms crowded and in need of painting, the bathrooms clean but fitted with ancient fixtures. The gym doubled as a cafeteria. A so-called multipurpose room that served as a makeshift auditorium actually had a couple of old, unused urinals along one wall.

But as Sameera walked through the crowded hallways and overheard the joking and chatting and arguing and complaining, she realized again how much she missed being with people her age. And unlike St. Matthew's students, who could effortlessly blend into the most formal of White House social events, there was nothing "traditional and timeless" about the scene at Jacob Lawrence. The atmosphere was electric, new, and fresh. Some people were pulling off a set-the-trend kind of style that Sameera figured would travel the planet in a couple of months. A few were so out there they were virtually sci-fi.

Mariam, it turned out, was a quiet but highly respected nerd, exactly as Sameera had anticipated. In her first class, the teacher looked even more bored than the kids as she droned on, reading verbatim from an ancient textbook about the Roman Empire. Next, a math teacher handed out worksheets and drowned out the din by putting headphones on and listening to music. Sameera glanced over the worksheet and was glad to see that she could finish it without any problems, thanks to Westfield's help.

Third came a PE teacher who picked two captains, ordered them to divide into teams, and left the class on the windy basketball court, while she ducked behind the gym to grab a smoke. The few guys who started a pickup game were the only ones who stayed warm, along with

Sandra—who raced around with them in her burka and scored two baskets. Sameera and her mother were fine, too, thanks to the thick wool they were wearing, but the rest of the class stood huddled together against the chilly wind.

Mariam's two best teachers came in a row right before the visitors left. The first taught history and made a discussion about the Civil War so interesting that Mom got carried away and raised her hand to answer a question. Sameera reached over and yanked on her burka, and Mom managed to shift the hand raising into a stretch yawn kind of motion.

"He's good," Sameera whispered to Mariam as they left the class.

"He treats us with respect," Mariam answered. "And gets it back."

Her last period before lunch was English, taught by a young woman who managed to maintain perfect order, even in a class of forty-some rambunctious, distracted students. She was tough and demanding, but the kids settled down and tuned into every word. Sameera listened carefully when Mariam was called to read her essay. The class had been assigned to review Khaled Hosseini's *The Kite Runner*, and Mariam's lyrical, concise description of the novel made Sameera decide immediately to read it.

Mariam took them into the principal's office before they left. Mr. Richards was a middle-age man who was built like he'd once been an athlete, but today he looked exhausted even though it was only noon. "We just got a shipment of computers from some company that wants a tax write-off," he said, pointing to about twenty huge cartons piled in the lobby. "The problem is that we don't have anywhere to put them and nobody has time to set them up."

Sameera checked out the boxes and recognized the brand name of the desktops immediately. *Wow*, she thought. *Those are some nice machines. I could make them HUM.* She noticed Sandra also taking a close look.

"I'm so glad your guests came to our school," Mr. Richards was saying. "I still think they should see some other American schools, though. Ours isn't typical, which is probably good."

Mom whispered something into Mariam's ear.

"My guest is wondering something. If you received a substantial sum of money for the school, how would you use it?" Mariam asked.

The principal grinned. "She wants me to dream big, huh? Well, I can do that. Our facilities are crowded and we don't have money for extracurriculars, but I know exactly how I'd spend a nice chunk of change—that is, if I had absolute power. I'd double my good teachers' salaries, and recruit some new people with vision and energy." He sighed. "You can translate that later, Mariam. For now, thank them so much for coming. I hope it was a valuable experience."

Mariam said good-bye at the door. "Call me later," she whispered to Sameera. "I want to know what your parents decide."

The three burka-clad women slid into the back of the getaway car. The moment they were safely around the corner, Sandra yanked off her head covering and cracked her window, even though the February air outside was frigid. "This head thing is suffocating," she said, panting like Jingle on a car ride. "How do they take it?"

"You get used to it," Sameera said, her voice still muffled under her veil. "Well, Mom. What do you think?"

Mom turned to face Sameera, and there was a definite sparkle in her fake brown eyes. "I think the First Lady might take on teacher salaries as another domestic focus. How does a Double Their Salaries Foundation sound, Sparrow?"

"You go, Mom. Sounds good to me."

"The best part is that we got to see the school without the fuss of a formal visit. I'm sure the teachers didn't change their style much—they thought we couldn't understand a word they were saying. We really got to see what that place was like."

"So what about *me*, Mom? Are you okay with me going to Jacob Lawrence now that you've seen it?"

"Yes, I am. And your father will be, too, I'm sure. But do you still want to go now that *you've* seen it? It's so crowded, and I heard a lot of rough language."

"I've heard worse, Mom. But you've cleaned up your act quite a bit since Dad became president."

Her mother grinned. "You should hear me vent in the shower when none of the White House staff can hear. Anyway, Sparrow, the kids seemed pretty nice on the whole. I don't get why we had to go through all that security at the entrance."

Sandra cleared her throat. "Assault with a knife two years ago," she said. "A boy was almost killed. It's safe now, though. That's a state-of-the-art metal detector they've got."

"Oh. There's no need to tell the president about ancient history, then, is there? Sparrow, what do *you* want to do? Would you like to study at Jacob Lawrence next year?"

"I'd love it, Mom. And the best part is that I already have a friend there. Isn't Mariam wonderful?"

"She is. And she's obviously a good all-around student, but she really shone in that English class, didn't she? When she read her essay out loud, you could tell that she loves to play with words almost as much as you do, Sparrow. When Ran goes back to Maryfield in June, you'll be glad to have a friend like Mariam around."

"You're right, Mom," Sameera said.

"We can ask the Secret Service office about having JB and Sandra on permanent assignment with you at school. I'll have no worries about your safety if the two of them are there with you."

"I'm all over it, ma'am," said Sandra. "But you couldn't pay me to put on one of these outfits again."

Mom fingered her own burka. "I'm holding on to mine," she said. "You keep yours, too, Sparrow. Who knows when we might need to go undercover again? It felt great to be out in public without every eye staring at me. A huge relief, actually. For the first time I see how some of my Muslim friends feel that wearing a burka can be a freeing thing. I'm not sure I agree, but at least I understand."

Sameera gazed out of the window as the taxi sped back toward the Treasury Building. *You don't really get someone until you've walked a mile in her burka,* she thought.

chapter 28

The next time Sameera visited the press room, John Malone cornered her after she was done chatting with a couple of bloggers. "It's got to be a book," he said.

"What?"

"Everybody's buzzing about your enrollment in public school, Sparrow."

"They are? But we haven't made our formal announcement yet. How do people know?"

"Come on, sweetheart. It's our job to ferret out a good story. The real mystery is *why* you're doing it."

"You're supposed to be the best in the business, Mr. Malone," she answered, smiling. "I'm sure it won't take you long to figure that one out." *Because I like to mix the old with the new. Because this First Daughter makes her own rules.*

John Malone shrugged. "Well, other motivations aside, I know you want to be a writer, love. I'm thinking a best-selling book about her year in a public high school, by Sameera Righton. And it would come out just when her dad's up for re-election."

"That's not a bad idea, Mr. Malone. Got any tips?"

"Only one. Write it like Pearl would. Listen, respect the people who've been there for generations, ask the right questions, and learn to speak their language."

Suddenly, Sameera felt like she was participating in a solemn commissioning ceremony. "I'll do my best," she promised.

Back upstairs, she collapsed into the recliner that had become unofficially hers. It wouldn't hurt to keep a journal of her year at Jacob Lawrence. Book or no book, it would be a great way to capture the excitement she was already feeling about the place.

"Ready to see my first movie, Sparrow?" Miranda called from the adjoining room.

"Right now? Are you sure *you're* ready?"

"Yes. It's not perfect yet, but I was telling Tommy how worried I am that you might not like it, and he said I needed to trust myself. And you."

Sameera got up and joined her cousin. "You've sure been talking to him a lot, Ran. Are you obeying his every command now?"

"Stop it, Sparrow. No, of course not. He asks me for advice, too."

"Really? Has he . . . said anything about going out?"

"You mean with me? No way. He treats me like a little sister. For now, at least. But I turn eighteen in less than a year, and I made sure to tell him that. Now, are you ready to see this?"

"Of course. I'm so excited, Ran."

The girls sat side by side in front of the computer and Miranda clicked the PLAY button. The film was titled simply: *January: The Rightons Move In.* She'd figured out how to switch color footage into black and white, and had paired it first with music that sounded like it had been lifted out of an old Charlie Chaplin film. Brief scenes faded in and out—a funny one of Sameera feigning delight at opening a big box and seeing Jingle leap out (she'd really hammed that one up for the camera). Mom and Dad dancing cheek to cheek in the empty State Dining Room as decorators repainted the walls. Sameera and Mom arguing over which wall in the family library should bear a big framed picture of the Maryfield clan. The mob of Rhinos who'd chased their limo down the street after they left church, shrinking and then disappearing into the distance. Sameera remembered how Miranda had turned to capture them with her camera that day.

The music changed in the last scene, shifting to an instrumental version of "Amazing Grace." And there was Dad, walking by himself in the State Room. He seemed lost in thought as he studied the paintings on the walls, stopping to gaze up at the enormous portrait of Abraham

Lincoln. Somehow, Miranda had manipulated the lighting until the quiet figure in front of the big painting dimmed and became a silhouette. And that's when the credits rolled, announcing in small letters that the film had been DIRECTED AND PRODUCED BY MIRANDA JANE CAMPBELL.

"Oh my," Sameera managed. "I want to see it again."

"Are you sure?" Miranda said, studying her cousin's expression anxiously. "You don't have to pretend for my sake, Sparrow. It's not totally finished yet."

"Shut up and let me watch it again."

After playing the three-minute film all the way through, Sameera turned to her cousin. "This. Is. Amazing," she said.

"Really? You really like it, Sparrow? You're not just saying that?"

"It's . . . beautiful. Hey, I've got a great idea. Let me post it on my blog."

"I thought of that. But what if we violate some kind of security rule, or the press office has a fit?"

"I don't think they'll mind. Oh no. They won't mind at all. If this film doesn't do wonders to raise President Righton's approval ratings, I don't know what will. It's so . . . us. It's real. It's not staged at all, and people will *get* that."

"All right, Sparrow," said Miranda. "If *you* think it's good enough. But let's get it cleared, okay? Where should we go first?"

"Dad, definitely. And then the press secretary's office and the Secret Service. Once those people give the green light, the First Lady's office won't have any objections. Besides, I already know Mom's going to love it. We'll use my laptop as a porta-theater. Let's go."

Dad was in a meeting with his Cabinet, so his secretary asked the girls to wait in the small study adjacent to the Oval Office. A few minutes later, the president came in, glancing at his watch.

"What's up, girls?"

"Give us five minutes, will you, Dad?" Once they got her father's permission to show the film publicly, nobody could stop them.

"Five minutes exactly. They'll start to get tense if I don't come back soon."

But once the film started playing, he watched it intently. "Miranda, you have a gift," he said. "I give it two thumbs-up. Now if you'll excuse me, girls—"

And he was off, leaving the cousins to fist punch each other and move on to their next destination—the press office.

The press secretary smiled her greeting. "Your blog's terrific," she told Sparrow. "Keep up the great work. Love the honesty. You're really connecting your father to the next generation."

"Thanks. We came down to ask you to take a look at my cousin's film. I'd like to post it on my blog, but we wanted to get your clearance first."

The press secretary was as delighted with Miranda's film as Sameera's father. "It's a go for me, girls," she said.

"Next stop, Secret Service," said Miranda. "I think I can handle that on my own, Sameera. And then I'll have to show the film to Tara and your mom. Why don't you take Jingle on a walk before he stains one of those antique rugs? We've completely neglected the poor pooch lately."

Sameera dashed upstairs to get Jingle before his bladder exploded and took him out to President's Park. When she stopped to throw a tennis ball for him on the South Lawn, JB came over to join them, and she couldn't help noticing that he was wearing a big grin. In fact, he was bubbling over with as much joy as the retriever. *If he had a tail, he'd be wagging it,* Sameera thought.

"Well, JB, you've obviously got some news. What's up?"

"It's all good, Peanut," he announced. "I told her everything—about the divorce, the kids, everything. And she wants to meet them."

"That's wonderful, JB," Sameera said, throwing the ball so that Jingle could retrieve it and feel great about himself. "What made you change your mind?"

He picked up the tennis ball and threw it far, far, far, and Jingle went roaring off into the distance. "It felt like we were meant for each other the first time we went out. And then I read your post on Sparrowblog, and—"

She interrupted. "You did?"

Maybe she should stop being surprised that people over the age of twenty-five were reading her posts.

"Yep. It's sort of addicting to read the comments. Any-way, I started thinking a lot about my own three treasures, and it hit me that Tara has all of them—she's strong, she's smart, and she's . . ." His voice trailed off, and Sameera could tell he was momentarily embarrassed.

Clearing his throat, he continued, "Anyway, she has the three bottom-line qualities I'm looking for, so I thought I'd better lay it all out with her. I mean I've got nothing to lose, do I? She's meeting the twins this weekend."

"And lots to gain. Let me know how it goes, okay? I'll be thinking of you."

chapter 29

Miranda was still downstairs hammering out the details of her film's release on Sparrowblog. What was taking her so long? Was somebody objecting to something in the movie? Sameera couldn't think of anything—she was still overwhelmed by how good her cousin's work was.

While she was waiting, she decided to end the discussion about nonnegotiables so that the blog was ready for a new post. She scrolled through the comments again and added up the most popular treasures mentioned, feeling great that her lighthearted post had spurred JB to action. Now it was time to confess her own three nonnegotiables. If only Bobby had gotten a chance to post so she could see his before she revealed hers. But what was this? Yes!

Another e-mail from Ghoshboy@zmail.com zinged into her in-box as though it had been summoned by her subconscious. She opened it quickly; she wanted to read it in private, especially if it was bad news about his grandfather.

```
Dear Sameera, You might want to know that
miracles do happen. I've told my grandfather
about you, and all is well.

I'd been reading him parts of your blog
aloud in the afternoons. He's always been
interested in politics, so he liked the fact
that your father is a public servant, and
that I met you during the campaign.

At first I left out any mention of you being
Pakistani, but I could tell he was getting
more interested in your situation as he
listened. "She sounds quite bright and
steady, Bobby," he said. "The perfect
president's daughter."

A couple of days later, I read him something
about your adoption. "Is she from another
country or is she American?" he asked.

I glanced at my father, and he gave me one
of those slight nods of permission. "She's
```

American now, Dadu, but she was born in Pakistan," I said.

Dadu looked right into my eyes. "And why didn't you tell me that from the start?"

Truth-telling time. Finally. "I know how you feel about Pakistanis, Dadu. I know you're sad about losing the family's land. And your brother. I wasn't sure how you'd feel about me having a friend who was Pakistani."

He was quiet for a minute. "Are you in trouble with this girl, Bobby?"

"No."

"Have you been meeting with her?"

"Not recently."

Silence again. "Why not?"

"Because I care what you think, Dadu," I said. "I wouldn't do anything to dishonor you."

That's when he took my hand and held it for a long time. "The war was sixty-some years

ago," he said after a while. "It's time to
forgive now, isn't it?"

"Yes," I said, and I saw my father wiping his
eyes with his handkerchief. My father. Who
never cries.

But then I wanted to be SURE Dadu didn't mind
me spending time with you. And maybe being
photographed, or making international
headlines. So I asked his permission to
court you. Right there and then.

(*You did? What does that mean in twenty-first century-speak?*
Sameera thought.)

Then, to my total amazement, he tilted his
head just like my father had minutes before.
In India, in case you didn't know, that means
yes, Sparrow. YES! And the best part was
that my father was in the room, so he saw
it, too.

Dadu doesn't have much longer, the doctors
say, so thank you for helping us have the
most honest conversation we've ever had in
our lives, Sparrow. He seems different, too,
lighter somehow. Less grumpy. I'm not as sad

about saying good-bye now that I know he's made his peace with the past.

I contacted G-Dub and explained my situation, and they said I can pull out for the rest of the semester and take summer school instead. But when the time comes to head back to the States, I've told my parents that I'm not flying back to Charleston with them. No, I'm flying into Dulles, and taking a taxi straight to the White House. I'm looking forward to being together, like a reward at the end of a race. Love, Bobby

P.S. I tuned into Sparrowblog before writing this. No time to post there, but here are my treasures, Sparrow: a soft heart, honesty, and understanding. I don't think I need to tell you that you've got all three.

Sameera read the whole thing again. And then again. She got up, got a box of tissues, and read it through one more time.

That's when she realized that in his postscript, he'd named his nonnegotiables, and that two of them exactly matched the ones she'd chosen. What was it that Senator Banforth had said? Something like "If your short list mirrors his, that's when you know he's a keeper. Even two out of three would be a good sign." And there they were in black and white—a soft heart, which obviously meant tenderness, and honesty. *And understanding?* she thought. *That's cake. I've got reams of that!*

She reread the entire e-mail over and over, and each time she fell a little more in love with the author. He was the guy of her dreams, and it was terrible not to be able to write him back and tell him how much she missed him. Maybe she could commandeer Air Force One and head straight to Kolkata to see him *right now.*

Things could have taken a different turn, she told herself, trying to keep such insane, passion-driven plans in check. *His grandfather could have said no to our relationship.* Well, that didn't matter now, did it? Happy endings did happen, and she wasn't going to second-guess this one. *Sorry, Romeo and Juliet. This pair of lovers won't have to choose between love, life, and family. Some of us get to have all three.*

She pulled herself out of her haze of romance to write the post.

Thanks to everybody who sent in responses to my "appraisal: fill in the blanks" post. If you leave off *hot* and *sexy*, which I plan to (sorry, Mrs. Graves!), two of your most popular answers were also on Sara Teasdale's list: *kind* (gentleness in her poem) and *funny* (humor in her poem). Tied with those two for the top three spots was *smart*. None of those made my top three, although I think they're all great. Mine are *honest, brave,* and, like Miss Teasdale herself, *tender,* in case you're still interested. I also heard from a wise woman that if two out of three of your nonnegotiables match your sweetheart's, consider the other person a keeper. Comments? Remember, keep them short, clean, and to the point. Peace be with you. Sparrow.

Her cousin came back, beaming. "I've got the green light," she said. "You were right, Sparrow. Everybody loved my movie. Your mom especially."

Sameera closed her laptop; she didn't intend to share this particular note from Bobby with anyone. She'd summarize it later for her cousin. "What took so long if they loved it?" she asked.

"Oh, Tara sat me down and drilled me about little kids. What they were like, how you got them to connect with you, stuff like that. She'd heard that I taught Sunday school for a couple of years. She must be planning an elementary school visit for Aunt Liz or something like that."

"Nope, that's not it at all. She's about to meet JB's kids."

"She is? Oh, that's wonderful! Seems like she's a bit nervous about it. I hope those kids like her, for his sake. *And* hers."

"Not to mention theirs. Now let's get busy posting that film, Ran."

chapter 30

The following Friday, Sameera left her cousin baking up a storm in the third floor kitchen that had become Merry Dude Dairy Farm Fresh Cookies headquarters and headed off to the SARSA meeting by herself.

Mariam had phoned to say she couldn't come to the meeting, so the ride to the café at the edge of GW's campus took only a few minutes. Sameera crawled out of the limo and was immediately blinded by a score of flashes. The Rhinos had followed her, just as she'd known they would. Her agents escorted her safely through the crowd, but several paparazzi trailed her inside.

This time, it took Sameera a while to locate her SARSA friends. She smiled and waved at people who called out her name as she pushed through the throng. Ah, there they were, clustered in a corner—Nadia, stunning as usual, Sangi, with her big, welcoming smile, George, jumping up to pull out a chair for Sameera.

"Hey, you're not in disguise," George said.

"Nope. I'm food for the media tonight, as you can tell. Get ready for an article or two about how you're the love of my life, Mr. George. So how's it been going with you guys?"

"Great," said Sangi. "We're hosting a guest speaker in a couple of weeks—that Republican, Indian American congressman who was just elected. He's young and hip and supposed to be the *new face of the party*."

"Nadia's wild about him," said George. "She's the one who invited him."

"He's married, you idiot," Nadia said, punching him on the shoulder. "Two kids. They've even got a turtle, for goodness' sake."

"What's a turtle got to do with it?" George asked. "And must you resort to violence?"

Sangi grinned. "Moving the conversation along," she said, "Miranda's movie's fantastic, Sparrow. We couldn't believe how good it is."

"The feedback so far has been fabulous," Sameera said. "The next one's going to be even better. She's got hours of footage of food in the White House. She might be using some scenes from our meeting in her third one, but only if you guys give permission, of course."

"I've got no objections to becoming a movie star," said Nadia, and that shiny cascade of hair agreed as it danced behind her.

"Me either," added George. "But I already have to fight the girls off. What's going to happen when my mug shows up on Sparrowblog? Or in the press?" Turning to face the photographers clustered in a corner of the café, he pursed his lips and flexed his biceps. Flashes exploded.

The girls ignored him. "There were lots of good follow-up comments on your post about treasures," said Sangi.

"Yeah," said George, "If you'd left in *sexy* and *hot,* most of the people who read Sparrowblog seem to want to go out with *MOI*. Ouch!"

Sangi had punched his other shoulder, but nowhere near as hard as he was pretending, reeling back in a slow-motion *Matrix*ish move.

"*Mine* were *smart, motivated,* and *confident,*" said Nadia, ignoring George's bad Keanu Reeves imitation. "I want a guy who respects himself and knows where he's going."

"I picked *smart,* too, and *tolerant,* and *honest,*" said Sangi.

"*Truthful* wasn't one of my top three," said George. "I picked *smart, fun,* and *adventurous.*"

"So if someone doesn't like hang gliding, you wouldn't go out with her?" Nadia asked.

"Well, *hot* was a close fourth for me, almost a tie, so I guess I'd give the anti–hang glider a date if she was extra babealicious."

"Where's Mariam tonight?" Nadia asked. "She's such a doll; I'm so glad you're going to start bringing her along to our meetings."

"She couldn't come tonight," Sameera answered. "But she definitely plans to. She so appreciates the way you guys have reached out to her. Which reminds me—my parents gave me the go-ahead to join her in public school."

"That's fantastic," George said.

"Wow, Sparrow, you're going to get all kinds of kudos in the press for this move," added Nadia. "I know that's not why you're doing it, but still."

"I'll be starting next fall, so get ready to read about it on Sparrowblog."

"Why next fall?" Sangi asked. "Why not right now?"

"My cousin's with me now," Sameera answered, startled by the question. "I wouldn't want to leave her in the lurch."

"Wouldn't it be easier to start now? Then the other kids might have a chance to get used to you. And by next year, you'd feel much more at home."

"Your cousin sounds really busy, anyway," Nadia added, a hint of jealousy in her voice. "Her film was great. She's got that cookie-making business, and I read somewhere that she and that gorgeous Tommy Banforth were caught having a romantic coffee somewhere in Georgetown."

"Oh, that. He was meeting with her to share some legal advice about setting up the cookie-making business. And copyright stuff about her film."

"Yeah, right," George said. "I think I'll go to law school."

"Maybe you guys are right about starting now," Sameera said thoughtfully. "I'll ask Ran what she thinks, and if she's okay with it, my parents just might give me the green light."

"Never hurts to try when it comes to the parental units," said Sangi.

The flashes were going off so fast now, she felt like they

were merging into a single strobe-light effect. *It's the Revolutionary Café and Disco,* she thought.

"I'd better go before we get headaches," she said, getting up. "Thanks for the idea, guys. I'll let you know what happens."

"Oh, Sparrow, I almost forgot," said George. "Here's a card from Bobby."

"You almost forgot?" Sangi and Nadia said it simultaneously.

George shrugged. "Yeah. He told me he didn't want to mail it to the White House because it would take too long to get through to Sparrow, so he sent it to me in another envelope instead. Express mail, I might add."

Sameera opened the sealed envelope the moment she was alone in her room, but she already guessed what it would say.

Dear Sameera,

I couldn't get to a cybercafé, but I wanted you to know that he's gone. I miss him, but something changed after we had that talk about you, and about forgiveness. He laughed more after that. He even cried once, telling me a story about his childhood and how his mother had sacrificed so much for him. I'd never seen him cry before, and neither had my Baba. It was a wonderful last few days with him. So thanks, Sameera. Thanks for that. I'll be home the last

week of March after the ceremonies are over. Keep us in
your thoughts and prayers.

Love,
Bobby

The card was one that he'd obviously made before leaving the States. It bore a photo of a soaring sparrow that had just taken off from the ledge of a skyscraper's window. The angle was from a higher window, so you could glimpse the bird's destination—a cozy nest tucked into an elaborate carving on the Gothic church below. Once again, the tiny initials BG in the lower right-hand corner revealed the identity of the photographer.

Sameera gazed for a long time at the sparrow soaring from a high, high building toward what was obviously home, and then she tucked the card in her desk along with the small stash of notes and keepsakes she knew she'd never throw away.

chapter 31

Miranda's movie became an instant hit. On Sparrowblog itself, which was getting more traffic than ever, comment after comment raved about it. Even Sparrowhawk admitted that she was glad to see such intelligent, personal coverage of the First Family. The film was getting a ton of buzz on the rest of the Web, too. It was quickly picked up by ifilmeditmyself.com and downloaded over and over again on different sites and blogs. It seemed like everybody who saw it was enjoying her intimate peek into life in the White House.

Maryfield folks, of course, were beside themselves with pride, and Miranda basked in the lavish praise she got from her parents and grandparents. The success of her first movie made her even more berserk for the camera. She was constantly filming, downloading megabytes of movie, and editing the footage as if she were on assignment for a major motion picture studio. *How the First Family Eats*, her second film, was scheduled to be finished in a few weeks, and she'd asked Sameera to announce the release date on Sparrowblog.

"This film has to be ten times better than the first, Sparrow," Miranda said. "People expect sequels to stink, so I'm trying to blow everybody away with mine. I've been researching info about film schools, and I'll want the admissions committees to see my best work."

"I'll post every film you make if you let me do something I've been wanting to do for a while now," Sameera told her cousin.

"Of course, Sparrow. Anything. Do you want to send Bobby's family some scotchies along with a sympathy card?"

"That would be great. But what I also want is Gaithers's card—the pleasure of shredding it."

Miranda looked sheepish. "I flushed it the day after you posted my film. The guy was a jerk, Sparrow."

"Definitely," Sameera said. Then she lowered her voice to make it sound like a reporter's: "This Academy Award winning movie was directed by Miranda Jane Campbell, who also owns the successful Merry Dude Dairy Farm Fresh Cookies business." She threw her arms around her cousin, kissed her, and then shifted back to her own voice. "I tell you girl, you're good at so much stuff, you're going to have to *choose* which talent will make you famous. I'm so proud of you."

"Thanks, Sparrow. It's been an amazing year so far, hasn't it?"

"It certainly has. Which reminds me, Ran. How would you feel if I enrolled in school right now?"

"Now? Why would you want to do that?"

"I figure it's going to take a while for them to get used to me, so the sooner the better. But I don't want to leave you here alone. I mean you came all the way to D.C. to be with me, and—"

"Listen, Sparrow. You've helped me follow my dreams this year. I'd be a bad cousin if I didn't let you follow yours. Maybe we can move my tutoring session with Westfield to the morning so that we can have the afternoons together. But you still have to talk Aunt Liz and Uncle James into an early start."

Sameera kissed her cousin on the cheek. "You're the best, Ran."

"I sure hope Tommy Banforth agrees with you."

"How about you and Tommy, Ran? Are you guys . . . falling for each other?"

"Nah. We're friends for now, but I'm working hard so that can change in a couple of years—like when I'm nineteen and he's twenty-three."

"I need to get to know him better then. He seems nice, but if he might be my future cousin-in-law . . ."

"Oh, you'll love him. He's got heaps of the three *F*s—he's so much fun to be with, he's got a strong faith and loves to go to church, and he's totally connected to his mom, grandparents, and cousins. We're a match made in heaven, Sparrow."

"Speaking of matchmaking, did you ever find out how it went with Tara and JB's kids?"

"No, but I'm *so* curious to see if she's still interested after meeting them."

As if on cue, a loud, demanding knock sounded at the door. *RAP! RAP! RAP!* "Some things never change," Sameera muttered, opening the door for her mother's right-hand woman.

Tara strode in as dynamically as ever, but Sameera thought she glimpsed something new in her face.

"I just wanted to tell you girls that Miranda's film might be featured on a major network soon," Tara said.

"Oh my gosh!" Miranda said. "I can't believe it!"

"It's an amazing PR tool," Tara added.

"You should probably start charging money for it, Ran. Pay per view or something," Sameera said.

"No way," said Miranda quickly. "These films are my thanks to you and your parents for having me here. I'm so glad to be helping in any way."

"Okay, then. I'll be heading home now," Tara said.

Sameera grinned and looked at her watch. "Already? It's only six o'clock."

That now-familiar pink flush came into Tara's cheeks. "I've got a date, girls," she said.

"With JB?"

"And the twins." She smiled at the expressions on the cousins' faces. "Oh, his kids are adorable. I love the way JB handles them—he's the world's best dad, that's for sure. He puts *their* needs first, which is how it should be."

"Sounds a lot different than Marcus Wilder," said Sameera, referring to Tara's old marketing geek boyfriend—the type who'd always put himself first.

"You can say that again. JB has all three of the treasures I'm looking for—he's strong, smart, and . . ." She stopped short, as though she'd already said too much, and Sameera noticed that her cheeks were fiery red now.

"Did you know that you and JB picked the exact same things?" she asked.

"I'm not surprised. 'If three nonnegotiables match, consider the other person a keeper.'" It was a quote from Sparrowblog, and after delivering it, Tara smiled again at the girls and left.

chapter 32

Listen up, Sparrowbloggers. For those of you who didn't catch the press conference on television, the big news is that I'm about to start school NOW—at **Jacob Lawrence High School** in D.C. I'm looking forward to it, but I've got the jitters, too. I know everybody worries about starting a new school, especially if you're doing it in the middle of your junior year when all the other kids know each other, but . . . well, this is different. I don't want special treatment and I don't want to stick out, but I'll have my agents with me and I'm sure reporters will be swarming the school on Monday. If that's not special treatment I don't know what is. Are you ready for me, Jacob Lawrence? Comments? Remember, keep them short, clean, and to the point. Peace be with you. Sparrow.

She didn't mention in her post that the school was public, but the first person to post a comment was Sparrowhawk. *Good for you, bird-girl*, was all it said, but it meant the world to Sameera.

The morning of her first day of school reminded her

eerily of the first day of kindergarten. Miranda tucked a homemade sack lunch and a bag of cookies into her backpack, Mom got teary-eyed when she thought nobody was looking, but Dad was the worst—just as he had been all those years ago. He came upstairs and stalked around while Sameera ate breakfast, offering nervous, useless advice like, "You've got to stand up to bullies," and, "Call me on your cell if you need anything." She almost expected him to tie her shoes for her.

Miranda helped her get dressed, pulling her hair back in a ponytail and choosing a pair of big gold hoop earrings, tight jeans, a black T-shirt with a dog outlined in pink sequins, and a white down parka. The three of them—and Jingle, of course—accompanied Sameera all the way to the East Entrance, where JB and Sandra were waiting by the armored car that would take her to school every day.

"Are you sure you don't want one of us to go with you?" Mom asked.

"I'll be fine, Mom. I'll stop by and see you after school and let you know how things went."

"I'll be around, too, Sparrow," Dad said. "Come have a coffee in the West Wing when you're done in the East Wing."

"Are *you* sure you're going to be okay, Ran?" Sameera asked, while Jingle circled the group as though trying to herd them back into the White House.

"I'll be fine," Miranda answered. "Westfield's coming, and then I have to fill three new orders for scotchies and work some more on that second movie. It'll be three o'clock before I blink."

A herd of Rhinos tracked the limo from the White House all the way to the stairway leading into the school. It was still early, but a few students were starting to push through the pack of paparazzi to climb the stairs. Even though she was fielding questions of her own, Sameera overheard a few other Q&A exchanges as she made her way up.

"How do you guys feel about the First Daughter coming to Jacob Lawrence?"

"Excited."

"Sort of scared. What if our school gets bombed by terrorists or something?"

"The first who?"

Just before entering the building, Sameera turned and waved and a barrage of flashes detonated around the semicircle of paparazzi.

The school looked cleaner, with fresh coats of paint everywhere. A huge banner hung over the door that read WELCOME, SAMEERA RIGHTON, and Mr. Richards was waiting to greet her.

This was the moment Sameera had been dreading, because she and Mom agreed that she needed to confess their burka disguise plan.

"You mean that was your mother?" he asked, dumbfounded. "Why didn't Mariam tell me? I would have done something special, I would have—"

"That's exactly why we didn't let Mariam tell you," Sameera said. "Mom wanted to see the school as is. And she must have liked it because she sent me back, right? But please, let's keep that secret visit just between you and me."

"Of course. We certainly don't want to stir up any more excitement around here. It's going to be hard enough to get any learning done over the next few days."

He was right. A constant stream of kids came up to Sameera to introduce themselves or to ask questions about life in the White House. Most of them didn't read her blog, she realized. She could always identify regular Sparrowblog readers because they didn't seem overawed by her presence or flustered by their brush with fame. Maybe the blog readers already felt connected to the First Daughter through the cyberconversations that progressed from week to week. But a lot of Jacob Lawrence students treated Sameera like a celebrity, asking for autographs, following her as she walked to class, badgering the agents with questions about their jobs, weapons, and training, and taking pictures with cell phones and cameras.

I'm glad I jumped into the deep end now, thought Sameera, signing yet another autograph in the hallway. *Probably by next fall, I'll be old news.* Still, even this first day would be interesting to describe later on her blog. And maybe, as she got to know some Jacob Lawrence students, she could ask them to share their stories with Sparrowbloggers.

The cafeteria was a prime location for informal photo

shoots. Both of the agents brought in their own lunches, and Mariam had *halal* food from home. She offered roti and lentils to Sameera, and Sameera, in turn, shared her cousin's White-House-made scotchies all around.

"Doesn't anyone at your school surf the Web?" she asked Mariam as kids came and went, asking if they could have their picture taken with Sameera or with one of the agents. "I'd love for these guys to read my blog. That would save me a lot of explanation."

"Some of us don't have computers at home," Mariam reminded her gently. "I read your blog at the public library."

"What about here at school?"

"We've got some computers set up but they're only for the teachers, and we don't have room for a computer lab. You saw those unopened boxes sitting in the hallway, right?"

"What about putting them in the library? I know it's small, but I think at least half a dozen computers could be squeezed around one of those tables."

"None of our teachers have time to set that up, and our librarian's only here two days a week."

"Why don't you and I help her, Mariam? I know something about setting up computers, and you're so smart, you'll figure it out in no time."

Mariam shrugged. "We could try, I guess. We can ask Mr. Richards. And the librarian's here tomorrow, so we can talk with her about it then."

The principal distractedly gave his permission, and the

librarian agreed. The school closed at three, but opened at seven in the morning to serve the kids who came in for a hot breakfast. Miriam and Sameera decided to work before classes started.

"We're going to need some help," Mariam said. "I'll get Rashida and Tahera to ask their linebacker boyfriends to come in early and lug the boxes over to the library."

She'd introduced Sameera to her two Pakistani friends, who spent most of their time attached to their boyfriends. The guys were neither Muslim nor Pakistani; somehow, Sameera couldn't imagine Rashida's and Tahera's parents ecstatically welcoming these boys into the family as potential husbands for their sixteen-year-old daughters. But maybe she was wrong. Nadia's parents were Pakistanis, too, and she was planning on taking a Filipino guy home with her for spring break.

"Do Tahera's and Rashida's parents *let* them date?" she asked Mariam curiously.

"No way," Mariam answered. "But they do it anyway, secretly. I could never go behind my parents' backs like that, could you?"

"I don't think so," Sameera admitted. *And thankfully, neither could the guy I love.*

Thanks to JB's and the boyfriends' muscles, the cartons of computers were moved to the library and the girls unpacked them. Setting up a network of eight terminals and printers on one small table was more complicated than Sameera had anticipated, but Sandra, who started as a technology specialist in the Service, helped out. A lot. Thanks to her (and a couple of extra items that Sameera paid for and smuggled in without anybody noticing), the new Jacob Lawrence network was soon up and humming.

chapter 33

The agents would have been a popular addition to the school even without Sandra's techno-skills. Girls flirted all the time with JB, despite the fact that he was twice their age. "It's that sexy earpiece," Tahera said, sighing as she watched him from afar. "And those dimples."

"He's taken," Sameera said hastily, catching sight of Tahera's boyfriend glaring at JB. "He's practically engaged to my mother's assistant."

More and more Jacob Lawrence students started visiting Sparrowblog now that they had access to the Web. So many kids wanted to use the computers that the librarian had to organize a sign-up sheet for fifteen-minute chunks of time.

Meanwhile, Sameera found most of the schoolwork easy to handle. A few of the teachers seemed a bit wary of her at first, as though they were afraid to grade or correct the First Daughter. But after a few days, when they realized she wasn't the diva type, they, too, settled down. She had some of her classes with Mariam, and she was glad that she'd been placed in the section with the inspiring English teacher.

Mariam shone in every subject. "I did fine on my practice SATs," she told Sameera. "Now if only I could show that I had more well-rounded activities than just helping my baba organize the inventory for his shop. Which reminds me, my grandmother keeps bugging me—she wants you to come back to our *ghar* for a visit."

"*Ghar?*" Sameera asked, remembering that Bobby had used the same word in his e-mail. "Doesn't that mean 'house?'"

"I think a better translation is 'home,' Sameera," Mariam said. "But your pronunciation is perfect—you've got that *gh* sound and the *uh* that follows it just perfectly."

"What's the word for '*white,*' then?"

"*Sa-fed.*"

"So, I live in the *Sa-fed Ghar?*"

"That's close enough," said Mariam, grinning. "Have you heard from Bobby about when he's coming back?"

By now, Sameera had discovered two wonderful things about Mariam: she was a great listener and she knew how to keep a secret. "Yes! Two more weeks until Bobby Return Day, Mariam. I can't wait!"

She was desperately and passionately longing for Bobby, night and day, week in and week out. He'd sent a quick note with his flight information, but after that, no e-mails came from that cybercafé in Kolkata, and Sameera totally understood why. He was grieving the loss of a grandfather. He was helping his parents settle the details of the funeral and estate, and reconnecting with family friends and second cousins. As she updated her countdown-to-BRD calendar on her laptop, ticking off another day, and then another, a part of Sameera wished she could be there with him, helping, getting to know his family, trying her best to be a comfort.

Soon, the cherry trees were putting out tentative buds. Birdsong filled the White House gardens, and the stately old trees were ready to be clothed again in fresh new leaves. Even the lawns were beginning to shift from a dull brown to a misty green.

And finally, finally, BRD arrived.

Sameera was waiting for him just inside the entry hall; she'd already called to make sure his flight was on time. Ran had helped her pick out her outfit, like she did for any special event—faded blue jeans, sandals, a thigh-length, white-and-blue embroidered kurta, and some bracelets of her own. *We'll make music together,* Sameera thought as she checked her watch for the thirtieth time and the bracelets clinked their accompaniment.

The taxi from the airport dropped Bobby off right outside the North Portico. He made it through the first round of security at the gate, and Sameera watched him from the entry hall as he walked up the circular driveway toward the steps. He'd dressed nicely for the long trip. She could see the oxford-cloth button-down blue shirt and beige slacks under his open coat, and a rolling suitcase trailing behind him. His hair was much shorter than it had been, but to Sameera's eyes, that made his chiseled features stand out even more.

And he was carrying flowers in his free hand—a dozen long-stemmed, old-fashioned, gorgeous red roses. Maybe it was the bouquet that did it, or the expression on his face as he scanned the façade of the White House. Sameera raced out into the crisp March air, stopping on the step just above him as they came face-to-face.

She'd been waiting so long for this moment and had rehearsed a hundred different sentences that would be perfect for their reunion. But in the moment, with Bobby six inches away, she found herself at a complete loss for anything to say.

A tenderness too deep to be gathered in a word. Sara Teasdale's last line of poetry came leaping into her mind as he cupped her face in his hands. She felt the familiar steel of a bangle graze her skin. Did she put her arms around him first, or did he kiss her first? It didn't matter. It wasn't a passionate kiss or a steamy embrace, but they looked into each other's eyes for a long minute afterward, and still neither of them said anything.

Then Jingle came hurtling through the open door, barking his welcome, and they heard Miranda yelling something as she followed the dog down the stairs.

"Hush, Jingle," Sameera said, pulling away from Bobby. "What's up, Ran?"

"Sorry for interrupting, but the agents want Bobby to go through security ASAP," her cousin said. "The guys on the roof thought he was attacking you. Hi, Bobby, by the way. It's great to finally meet you."

"Me too, Miranda, but I feel like we've known each other for a long time already."

"Thanks to Sparrowblog," Miranda said.

"Thanks to Sparrow," Bobby said, his eyes going back to Sameera's face.

"I was so sorry to hear about your grandfather, Bobby," Sameera said.

"It was hard. I want to tell you about his memorial service," Bobby said. "We have so much to talk about. How long does security take?"

"It shouldn't take long at all," Sameera said, taking his hand and leading him up the rest of the stairs.

"That is if you're playing by the rules," Miranda added, waiting for Sameera to join her. They launched into the list together:

"You didn't bring any animals, oversize backpacks, balloons, beverages, chewing gum, electric stun guns, fireworks or firecrackers, food, guns or ammunition, knives with blades over three inches or eight centimeters, mace, nunchakus, cigarettes, or suitcases along, did you?"

"Just one suitcase," he answered, smiling at the cousinly

harmony. "But it's full of presents for you and your family. I even brought something along for the pooch. They can x-ray it if they like, but I don't want them unwrapping anything, okay?"

"White House rules are pretty strict, but we'll figure it out," Sameera said, throwing open the doors to the entry hall. "Welcome to *my ghar,* Bobby. Make yourself at home."

chapter 34

Mariam and Sameera were walking by the computer lab, where a constant buzz of students and teachers could be heard from the hall.

"So, when can I meet Bobby?" Mariam asked. "You're glowing so brightly we might as well turn off the lights."

"Come home with me after school on Friday. Miranda and I are going to plan my seventeenth birthday party, and we want you to help. He's coming that night with the rest of the SARSA gang."

"I'll ask my father. He lets me go to the meetings because he thinks it will help me get into the university. It's my only after-school activity."

"I've got a great idea for another extracurricular, Mariam," Sameera said. "You can be cofounder and editor-in-chief of the *Jacob Lawrence News.*"

"What? I told you, we don't have a newspaper here, Sameera."

"We're going to start one. An online one that won't cost the school anything more than the price of the domain name, which is crazy cheap. This school needs a paper—kids love reading about themselves, trust me. It builds school spirit."

"Hmm . . . you might be right. I'll talk it over with Mr. Richards."

On Friday afternoon, Miranda, Sameera, and Mariam gathered in the Lincoln Sitting Room, accompanied, of course, by the faithful Jingle. "We're going to throw a great party for you, Sparrow," Ran said. "You don't turn seventeen every day, you know."

"I missed your party because of the campaign," said Sameera. "What makes me so special?"

"Besides being the best First Daughter ever?" Miranda asked.

"Yeah, besides that."

Miranda planted a big kiss on her cousin's cheek. "Because you're so cute, you idiot."

"We've got to plan this carefully," Mariam said. "People everywhere are going to find out about it. First things first. Who's on your guest list, Sameera?"

"The three of us. And the SARSA gang. And Tommy . . ."

"What about some of the other students from school?" Mariam asked. "They've all been dropping hints left and right to come and see this place."

"That's it!" said Sameera.

"How are you going to choose who gets to come?" Miranda asked. "Isn't it a huge school?"

"We'll invite the entire junior class," said Sameera. "That way nobody gets left out."

"I'm up for that," said Miranda. "Okay, we've got to (a) convince your parents—which means another good Sunday night family dinner; (b) tell the security dudes; and (c) plan the fun. Let's get going on task C, girls. Tommy's best friend from high school is a DJ, and Tommy says he can get this whole building shaking."

"I'm a little scared about this party," Mariam confessed.

"Why? Think your dad won't let you come?" asked Miranda.

"No. It's that . . . I've never danced before."

"Don't worry, Mariam, you can go out to the dance floor with George. He's so extra-uninhibited that just being in his aura is relaxing."

"Yeah," said Miranda. "And then you'll be laughing so hard that everybody will *think* you're dancing."

When the SARSA crew arrived, it took all of Sameera's self-control to stay focused on the task of hosting, because Bobby was *definitely* "courting" her. He was holding her hand, pulling out her chair at dinner, brushing her hair out of her eyes, and sitting extra close on the antique sofa. He seemed oblivious to the fact that everybody else was stiffly and carefully avoiding staring at them, but Sameera and

Miranda exchanged a look of desperation as the conversation struggled to move along.

"Okay," Sameera said. "Let's talk about the elephant in the room."

"Finally," George said. "When did you guys . . . become a thing?"

Sameera and Bobby took turns explaining the story, and more than one person in the room reached for a tissue as he shared about his grandfather letting go of old bitterness.

After that, the air cleared, the elephant disappeared, and they ended the evening ensconced in the red velvet chairs of the theater watching a hilarious Bollywood flick that Sangi had brought along.

chapter 35

Spending time with Bobby wasn't the only thing keeping Sameera busy that spring. The *Jacob Lawrence News* got the green light from Mr. Richards, and he even allocated money to provide a top-notch camera. Mariam invited a couple of excellent artists in the school to help with design, and two computer-savvy kids, tutored by Sandra, used their artwork to set up the template. Three good writers joined the team, one to cover sports, one to feature entertainment reviews, and another investigative-journalist type who didn't mind tackling controversy.

When the first issue went live, students and teachers logged in throughout the week, leaving comments on the many interactive areas the staff had created in the paper. Mariam decided to run interviews, and she had a knack with Q&A that made her "student of the week" sound fascinating, even if he or she wasn't the most popular kid in school.

Sameera joined the team when they worked in the mornings or at lunchtime, but she stuck to copyediting or contributing brief blurbs here and there. She wanted to save some creative energy for later, when she stayed up late writing a new post, or composing the next chapter of her book.

She loved writing about Jacob Lawrence on Sparrowblog— she shared their progress in setting up the paper, ranted about her ongoing vendetta against trigonometry (*why* did a journalist need to know that sine-squared theta plus cosine-squared theta equals one?), and described the tight sense of community shared in various circles. Lots of the Spanish-speaking students were second and third cousins, and most of the African-American kids had grown up attending Sunday school together in a big church on the corner. Sparrowbloggers also read about some of the harder things going on at the school, like the fact that some ethnic groups didn't mix it up at all. And how a couple of her classmates disappeared for days on end without any news. Sameera even wrote a post on behalf of a group of girls who were lobbying the district to provide a nursery on campus so they could bring their babies to school with them. They got the funding.

But she also felt free to write about the glam and glitz of life in the White House. After all, events like chatting with the secretary of state about crew (he'd rowed for Harvard) or waltzing with an Olympic athlete were parts of her life, too. Sparrowbloggers seemed to enjoy the account of the private party at a senator's mansion in Maryland where an ancient-but-still-famous rock band flew in to perform. They got to read about the top thirty high-tech movers and shakers joining the First Family to laugh hysterically at Dad's favorite comedian. They found out about Sameera's private lunch with a few of the White House bloggers and the nuggets of wisdom she'd gleaned from that discussion. Sameera was discovering that even sharing a list of swag in an event goodie bag could be fascinating if written in just the right way.

And she wasn't the only member of the First Family to be hitting her stride. James Righton worked tirelessly, except for Sundays, of course, when he worshipped in the mornings at church and relaxed with his family for the rest of the day. First Lady Elizabeth Campbell Righton was almost as busy as the president. Her NACWAH initiative was thriving, she was bustling around trying to increase teachers' salaries, and her refugee advocacy work overseas was still going strong. She was also now a regular member of Senator Banforth's bipartisan women's Bible study.

And what about the First Lady's extremely competent right-hand woman? Tara was working a lot less these days. She was so head-over-heels for JB that she was taking parenting classes and had been caught red-handed reading *The Thirtysomething Bride's Guide to Marriage at Midlife*.

Miranda's cookie-making business had taken off; she was getting orders from all over town for events and special deliveries. The small kitchen on the third floor was now stocked with baking goods, cardboard boxes that held a dozen scotchies exactly, wax paper, and mailing supplies. Gallons of fresh milk arrived in droves from Merry Dude Dairy Farm. And when Miranda wasn't baking or studying with Westfield, she was in the thick of making movies three and four. She'd bought more memory, batteries, and other camera gadgetry with her cookie money, but she was also squirreling away a lot of her earnings in a savings account.

What with everything they were doing, it was hard to find time to plan Sameera's seventeenth birthday bash. But when the big day finally arrived, the entire event took place without a hitch.

Sameera's parents agreed to stay upstairs in the Residence. "We'll celebrate with you on Sunday," Mom told her. "Having the president and First Lady show up at a party for young people could kill the atmosphere."

Sandra and JB worked out a hand-stamp security

procedure that would allow the kids to get inside quickly for the party. They cleared all the names on the guest list before the party and stamped their hands at school that day. Only people with hand stamps and identification were allowed into the White House for a quick second security clearance.

"Wear what you'd wear to a Jacob Lawrence dance," Sameera told everybody. "And no presents whatsoever. They won't let you bring them through security anyway."

The night of the party, Miranda, Mariam, and Sameera waited anxiously in the East Room. It seemed so formal and big. Famous, rich, and powerful people had feasted and danced in this space. And now the junior class of Jacob Lawrence High School was about to commandeer it.

More and more kids started passing through the entry hall. At first, they entered the East Room a bit hesitantly, but Tommy's friend the DJ made them comfortable right away by telling jokes and playing an upbeat mix of tunes. The three girls made sure everyone was greeted and welcomed.

"Happy Birthday, Sparrow," each guest remembered to say, and some of them hugged Sameera as though they'd known her for years.

"Let's get this party started!" Miranda said, and the cousins exchanged their signature fist punch before she went searching for Tommy.

Mariam let George lead her out to the dance floor, looking nervous but determined. Nadia had brought her boyfriend along, and they were standing so close you couldn't tell whose jeans belonged to whom. Sangi was having a great time dancing with Jean-Claude, the valet, who was singing the words to the reggae tune the DJ was playing.

Sameera watched Tahera and Rashida dancing with their boyfriends, Tommy showing off for her cousin (and vice versa), and George making Mariam giggle at his silliness. Suddenly, she remembered how much fun she'd had at the traditional Viennese Ball so many weeks earlier. She'd felt right at home that night amidst the classical music and formal gowns. Now her seventeenth birthday party was taking place in the same venue. This time, though, skin glistened with sweat as everybody jammed to a mix of hip-hop, reggae, *and* bhangra tunes. And she knew she was going to have as much fun as she'd had all those weeks before—if not more.

"Is your party all you hoped it would be?" Bobby asked, coming up beside her.

"Definitely," she said, reaching up to kiss his cheek. "Because you're here."

"That's not why you're loving it," he answered, smiling. "It's because you know how to feel at home anywhere, Sameera. And the best part is that you take everybody else there with you."

"Then what are we waiting for?" And just as she had the first day they'd met, she grabbed Bobby's hand and pulled him into the circle of dancing people.